You'll ne—

Talented Harlequin Blaze author Debbi Rawlins
makes all your cowboy dreams come true with her
popular miniseries

Made in Montana

The little town of Blackfoot Falls
isn't so sleepy anymore...

In fact, it seems everyone's staying up late!

Get your hands on a hot cowboy with

#837 *Anywhere with You*

(March 2015)

#849 *Come on Over*

(June 2015)

#861 *This Kiss*

(September 2015)

*And remember, the sexiest cowboys are
Made in Montana!*

Dear Reader,

The idea for this book took an interesting turn when I started to plot it out. In the second book of the series, the hero, Noah, was the sheriff of Blackfoot Falls. Since he's leaving Montana and joining the Marshal Service to be near the woman who stole his heart, the town needed a new sheriff. So I figured it was time to bring someone in and make him the hero of *Anywhere with You*. A friend, another writer who often plots with me, asked if I'd considered making the heroine a sheriff. I loved the idea and decided to let it float around in my head for a while.

I live in a small town in central Utah not much bigger than Blackfoot Falls. The week after my friend made her suggestion, I stopped at the clinic, and sitting in the waiting room was a deputy. I try to walk the straight and narrow, so I'm not acquainted with local law enforcement and had never met this deputy. But I asked if I could bother him with a few questions, and he was a great sport about it. We'd talked for a bit before I told him I was thinking about having a woman sheriff. The flicker of surprise in his face and the fleeting expression that said, "you're kidding" pretty much sealed the deal.

I hope you enjoy Grace and Ben's story as much as I enjoyed writing it. Did I mention that the deputy I met had the most arresting blue eyes?

Sincerely,

Debbi Rawlins

Debbi Rawlins

Anywhere with You

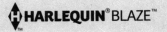

Recycling programs
for this product may
not exist in your area.

ISBN-13: 978-0-373-79841-4

Anywhere with You

Copyright © 2015 by Debbi Quattrone

Printed in U.S.A.

Debbi Rawlins grew up in the country and loved Westerns in movies and books. Her first crush was on a cowboy—okay, he was an actor in the role of a cowboy, but she was only eleven, so it counts. It was in Houston, Texas, where she first started writing for Harlequin, and now she has her own ranch...of sorts. Instead of horses, she has four dogs, five cats, a trio of goats and free-range cattle on a few acres in gorgeous rural Utah.

Books by Debbi Rawlins

HARLEQUIN BLAZE

Made in Montana
Barefoot Blue Jean Night
Own the Night
On a Snowy Christmas Night
You're Still the One
No One Needs to Know
From This Moment On
Alone with You
Need You Now
Behind Closed Doors

To get the inside scoop on Harlequin Blaze and its talented writers, be sure to check out blazeauthors.com.

All backlist available in ebook format.

Visit the Author Profile page at Harlequin.com for more titles

1

BLACKFOOT FALLS 26 MILES.

Ben Wolf smiled when he saw the warped metal road sign up ahead. No one had bothered to replace it, and now, fifteen years later, it still bore his mark—the large dent made by his baseball bat the day before he'd left town. He'd been leaning out of his friend Buster's pickup going thirty-five miles per hour when he'd taken a swing, and nearly dislocated his shoulder.

He'd been so damn angry that day. At his mother for all the lies, at the father he could barely remember, at the McAllister brothers for being better than him. Sure, the family had accepted him as if he'd been one of their own—and not *only* their maid's son—but that still didn't make him a McAllister.

Ben pressed down on the accelerator as he passed the sign and steered the Porsche into the curve in the highway. He hadn't thought about that day in years. Hell, he'd dislocated both shoulders since then, busted his ribs more times than he could recall and broken his jaw twice. The difference now was he got paid damn well to risk the occasional visit to the ER.

The sky was blue and cloudless, the air pleasantly warm considering the April sun was headed for the Rockies, their peaks still packed with snow. Patches of the mountainside below the tree line were still bare. Another month and the spring leaves would take care of that.

Northwest Montana was beautiful country. No argument there. In a way, Ben had been lucky to grow up on the Sundance. The ranch spread right up to the foothills, where clear water flowed in streams carrying all the fish a kid could catch. How many times had he fallen asleep in a grassy meadow, lulled by the warmth of the sun and the smell of wild sage?

Ben rolled down his window and breathed in the crisp, clean air. He watched a hawk wheeling and soaring through the sky. He hadn't realized how much he'd missed the mountains. Working as a stunt man, he'd seen plenty of great spots all over the States, Canada and Mexico. Even Europe once for an indie film. But nothing could beat the scenery here.

Hollywood had hills. Some nice views. And the city had other charms. But after living there for so many years, the glitter and sparkle had started to dim.

Maybe if everything went okay with his mother, he'd stick around for a week. Claudia had warned him their mom had aged. His sister saw her a couple times a year. All Ben had managed since leaving were phone calls at Christmas and sometimes on her birthday.

Distracted by his thoughts, he didn't swerve in time to avoid a rut in the road. The two right tires hit the packed dirt and sent dust flying everywhere. Ben cursed a blue streak for all the good it did. He'd gone an hour out of his way to have the Porsche washed and waxed in Great Falls. Just so it would be nice and shiny when he pulled into the Sundance.

Half the population of Blackfoot Falls would be there for Rachel McAllister's wedding, including a number of folks who thought Ben would never amount to anything. Let 'em see he'd done well for himself. Few things screamed success louder than a shiny red Porsche.

He peered at the road ahead, then glanced in the rearview mirror. The dust hadn't settled. A brisk breeze sent the airborne dirt swirling across the highway and chasing behind him. He accelerated, hoping that once he drove past the clearing, the scrubby brush would block some of the wind.

Taking another look in the mirror, Ben saw a flashing red light through the dusty haze. A second later, he heard the distinct blare of a siren.

A cop? Way out here?

"You gotta be kidding," he muttered, tempted to floor the accelerator.

The white truck had to be county-issue. Too old to keep up with his Porsche. Hell, his sports car had to be the only one around for miles. They'd catch him sooner or later. With his luck, a deputy would cuff him at the wedding.

Right. A deputy.

Not highway patrol. This was a county road.

Ben smiled as he pulled off to the side. Chances were damn good he'd gone to school with whoever was driving that truck. Kids from Blackfoot Falls rarely left after graduating. They normally stayed to work on the family ranch or found local jobs.

After turning off the engine, he stared into the rearview mirror and waited. The truck stopped several yards behind him. He couldn't make out the driver. Only that he was wearing a blue ball cap, which was odd. The sheriff and deputies had always worn Stetsons.

The truck door opened.

Ben turned his gaze to the larger reflection in his side mirror. The deputy was a woman. Medium height, slim, her tan uniform shirt tucked into snug-fitting jeans that showed off a small waist and curvy hips.

She closed the door and slowly approached him. Her

hair was pulled back, the color somewhere between brown and auburn. Sunglasses covered half her face, but he didn't think he knew her. He would've recognized her walk. Few women carried off that easy sensual sway. In his experience, it worked only if a woman was unaware of it.

Now, the ticket book in her hand he recognized immediately. Man, he did not need another mark on his record. His insurance premium had shot through the roof with the last ticket. But all wasn't lost. Lucky for him, he had a way with women.

"Good afternoon," she said with a small nod. "License and registration, please."

He removed his sunglasses, hoping she'd do the same. "Deputy Hendrix," he said, glancing at the name tag fastened just above her left breast. Then he gave her a slow lazy smile. "Is there a problem?"

Her lips parted slightly. "Really?" One corner of her mouth quirked up. "You're going to pretend you weren't speeding?"

At the unexpected response, Ben's smile faltered. "Not by much."

Her brows rose over the dark lenses, and she smiled a little. Not necessarily in a good way. "License and registration."

Jesus. Here they were in the middle of nowhere and she was going to push the issue? Ben dug out his wallet and then rifled through his glove box. He was getting to be a pro at this, he thought wryly, and handed over everything.

"Thank you," she said, her politeness annoying as hell.

Trying to keep his cool, Ben watched her step back and study his license. A faint sprinkling of freckles across her nose made her look young, probably midtwenties. If she'd gone to school in Blackfoot Falls, she would've been quite a few grades behind him.

"I know you, don't I?" he said.

The deputy looked up. "I doubt it."

Blue. He'd bet that was the color of her eyes behind the dark glasses. "Blackfoot Falls High?" He tried out another smile. "Obviously, I was ahead of you."

She cocked her head to the side. "So you're from here and know better than to go racing around these curves. Deer could come out of the brush at any time."

Irritated, Ben snorted. "You giving me a ticket or a lecture?"

"Both, if necessary."

So much for laying on the charm. He knew for a fact she hadn't been following him because he would've seen her. That meant she'd been parked off to the side. "You didn't clock my speed."

"And you know this how?"

"A hundred bucks says you don't have radar in that piece of crap you're driving."

She flipped open her ticket book. "You want to add gambling and harassment to the traffic violation? Be my guest."

"Come on...can't you just give me a warning? I'm only going to be here a few days." He noticed her slight hesitation, toying with her pen and angling her wrist to see her watch. Probably getting off shift soon. "I swear I'll drive like a nun."

That almost got a smile out of her. She held up his license for another look. "Mr. Wolf, you weren't just speeding a few miles over— Do you even know how fast you were going?"

Deciding to plead the fifth, he kept his mouth shut.

"You're lucky I don't bump this up to reckless driving."

His sigh came out low and desperate. "Don't do that," he said. "Please."

It about killed him to get the word out. And she knew it. Which probably told her too much about his lousy driving record.

"Look," she said, her voice softening. "I'm not trying to jam you up—"

The sound of a rough engine in need of a tune-up made them turn. A truck cruised down the highway toward them. White. Probably another sheriff's department vehicle. Could be good news for Ben if he knew the driver. But something she'd said had distracted him. *Jam you up?* She wasn't from around here.

He watched her mouth tighten and her shoulders go back. Nice high breasts. He couldn't help noticing. Also, that Deputy Hendrix didn't look happy.

"I won't cite you for reckless driving," she said, clicking her pen and opening her ticket book. "Just speeding."

Shit. He'd thought he had her...

The truck slowed.

She kept her head bowed, ignoring the driver.

So did Ben. He was too busy watching her nibble her lower lip. She didn't seem nervous so much as irritated.

Finally, she glanced over her shoulder. Her hair was pulled into a tight braid, all but a few wisps fluttering in the breeze. "Need something?" she asked.

"Nope." It was a male voice.

Ben dragged his gaze away from her, but too late to see who was in the truck. All he caught was a glimpse of the driver's tan uniform shirt as he drove off. Hell, it might've been someone Ben knew, and he could've saved himself this headache.

Deputy Hendrix resumed filling out the ticket. "I'm writing this for only ten miles over. Consider it a gift."

"Right."

She stopped and looked up, her eyes meeting his over the top of her sunglasses. Oh yeah, they were blue. As blue as the Montana sky. And brimming with annoyance at his sarcasm.

He smiled. "Thank you, Deputy."

She tore the ticket out of her book and handed it to him along with his license and registration.

She smiled back. "You have a real nice day, Mr. Wolf."

GRACE HENDRIX STOOD under the shade of a cottonwood tree, knowing she didn't belong. Not here at the Sundance ranch. Not at the wedding. And not in Blackfoot Falls. Yet here she was, trying to hold on to a smile while staring at all these strange, happy faces.

The bride, Rachel McAllister, had been kind to invite her, but Grace didn't really know Rachel. Or her three brothers. Or anyone else in the crowd of over four hundred people, all the women wearing dresses except, of course, Grace. If she still owned a dress, it was in storage along with most of her stuff. She'd packed in a hurry before leaving Arizona two weeks ago. Who knew what she'd crammed into the boxes?

Grace cast a quick glance at the two bars set up on either side of the huge white tent erected for the occasion. Her uncle Clarence was around somewhere, irritating someone, no doubt. Of that, Grace was quite certain. He was her mom's brother, the mayor of Blackfoot Falls, and the main reason Grace had moved to town, even though she didn't know him well. The last time she'd seen Clarence was at her mom's funeral. Grace had been ten. And while she appreciated his support, he was embarrassing her with his blatant campaigning to get her elected sheriff in November, so she'd given him the slip about an hour ago.

The shade inched away with the sun, and Grace inched along with it. The weather was perfect. Bright. Warm. People had scattered, gathering wherever they could find shade instead of confining themselves to the tent. This made escaping tricky. But everyone was busy laughing and talking, so it was possible she could dash to her car without being noticed.

She spotted Roy and cringed. He stood with his wife,

and luckily was more interested in the bowls of munchies at the bar than anything else, including Grace. Fine by her. She wasn't interested in socializing with him or the other deputies, though she hadn't seen any of them at the wedding. They probably hadn't been invited. Which meant they'd have something else to hold against her. As if being an outsider and a woman weren't enough.

She could hardly blame them. The sheriff had resigned. Noah would be gone in ten days, and she wasn't the only deputy who wanted to take his place. In truth, the others had a right to view her as an interloper, regardless of the fact she was the best qualified. Just like she had a right to throw her hat into the ring.

Someone tested the mic, drawing everyone's attention to the stage. Perfect opportunity for Grace to zip to the parking area. She pulled her cell out of her pocket and checked the time. It was already six. Preparing to bolt, she glanced toward the large three-story family home to make sure she wasn't being observed.

"Well, look at that."

The voice startled her. Grace whirled around, ready to make an excuse, when she saw it was three of the bridesmaids talking to each other. They weren't even looking at her.

"Where? What?" The blonde in the royal-blue dress shaded her eyes, her gaze darting from the stable to the house.

"Right over there," Katy said, her steady focus almost predatory. Grace had briefly met the tall brunette. She and the other two bridesmaids were Rachel's sorority sisters, all of them wearing different styles and colors of dresses, which Grace thought was pretty cool. "He just got out of the red Porsche."

Red Porsche?

Grace's heart skittered from first to third in two seconds. Silly, since she'd guessed the speed demon was in town for the wedding.

"I still don't see him." The shorter blonde wearing emerald green—Grace thought her name might be Chloe—pushed up on tiptoes. "Where?"

"Tall, longish dark hair? He's gorgeous." The blonde in blue adjusted her neckline, tugging at it until her cleavage was just so. "I wonder who he is."

"I bet he's Hilda's son," Katy said. "Ben, I think."

"Hilda?"

"You know...the McAllisters' housekeeper. Rachel said he was driving from California." Katy slid an arch look at the woman still fussing with her dress. "By the way, Liz, I saw him first, so don't even think about it."

It took a moment for Grace to realize she'd joined the pack and was actually waiting for a glimpse of Ben Wolf. If he spotted her, she wondered how he'd react. She knew he hadn't expected her to ticket him. A hot guy like that probably got away with murder.

Admittedly, her intention had been to give him a warning. Stopping him had almost made her late for the reception. But once Roy had seen them, she'd had little choice but to write the ticket. The last thing she needed was to come off as a pushover for a good-looking guy.

"California, huh?" Chloe settled back on her heels and drained her margarita. "I wonder what he does."

"Stunt man," Katy murmured. "He grew up here, though."

Chloe let out a laugh. "How do you know all this?"

"I overheard Hilda and Rachel's mom talking in the kitchen. Now that I think about it, Rachel mentioned him back in college." Katy straightened. "There he is. Walking toward her and Matt near the stage. Navy blue shirt. About six foot two. You can get a closer look when his arm's around my shoulder."

Grace smothered a laugh. But Katy had a good eye for

details. According to his driver's license, Ben was thirty-three and six foot two and weighed two hundred pounds. The sexy hazel eyes Grace had seen for herself.

A pair of stocky cowboys wearing Stetsons blocked her view. She moved slowly to the left. But caught only the briefest glimpse of him. She shuffled over a couple feet. And bumped into someone.

"Excuse me," she said, spinning around to see who she'd...

It was a tree. Jeez.

Chloe turned and smiled.

Grace smiled back and pretended she'd been on her phone. This took crazy to a new low. She was hanging around just to get another look at the guy. Even if she was interested, which she wasn't, Ben Wolf wouldn't give her the time of day unless he wanted something. Her instincts said this guy was trouble, and her cop gut was rarely wrong. Which meant she needed to keep her distance. She couldn't afford a misstep.

She'd come to Blackfoot Falls for a fresh start. To get her career back on track. To escape the lingering suspicion that she'd been involved in the death of her partner. Wrong place, wrong time was basically how Internal Affairs had ruled the tragic incident. But not everyone had believed her story.

Sighing, she slipped her cell into her pocket. Her car key was in there, as well as some lip balm. She hated carrying a purse. T.J. used to tease her about her stuffed pockets.

Damn. She couldn't think about her ex-partner right now. It would only depress her.

She needed to make the most of this opportunity at a fresh start and stop second-guessing herself. Stop worrying that moving here wasn't the answer. She'd deal with Uncle Clarence later. Make him see his nepotism was narrowing her odds of being named interim sheriff, much less getting elected in November.

"I should go see if Rachel needs anything." Katy looked over her shoulder, spotted a tray and set down her empty flute.

Liz snorted. "Good luck."

Grace's sweep of the crowd stopped dead when she got a perfect view of Ben. He looked like he'd walked off the cover of *American Cowboy.* The confidence practically oozed out of him. While he wasn't the only man wearing jeans, he seemed the only one who'd be comfortable wearing a tux to a softball game. It wouldn't matter. Women would flock to him either way.

Yep. Trouble. No two ways about it.

Katy was almost at her target. Just a few more steps—

"There you are, Gracie." It was Clarence. Hurrying toward her.

Terrific.

She dug deep for a smile. Why hadn't she stayed home? Oh, wait. She didn't have a home anymore. Just a small room at The Boarding House inn.

2

BEN HAD EXPECTED a few changes in Blackfoot Falls. Like the new filling station near the restored inn where he was staying. A pawn shop had replaced a burger joint. There were probably more surprises…he'd only stopped in town to check in and grab a shower. But damn, he never thought the Sundance would change. The ranch seemed smaller than he remembered. Both barns needed new roofs. And the east barn needed a coat of paint.

Granted, fifteen years was a long while, but in a hick town like Blackfoot Falls, time and people were supposed to stand still.

As Ben drifted through the wedding crowd, he recognized a few faces, but was unable to put names to them. Several old-timers nodded as he passed. Most of the guests just stared. He wondered if they remembered him or thought he was simply another stranger.

Sure, he'd grown up here right alongside the McAllister boys, gone to the same school with Cole and Jesse, played the same sports, shared a love of horses with Trace. But Ben had never been one of them. How could he have been when half the town never let him forget he was the maid's son. The other half just thought he was trouble.

He slipped off his sunglasses and stopped at a bar, or

rather, a folding table set up with booze, a keg and glasses for people to help themselves. So typically Blackfoot Falls and so different from his Hollywood life of excess and decadence.

He poured himself a scotch, neat, thinking about how he'd been a mere kid when he'd left, barely eighteen. Not old enough to drink legally. Of course, a small thing like breaking the law had never stopped him. He tossed back the scotch, feeling the burn all the way down, then left the glass on the tray with the others to be washed. He needed food in his empty belly, not more alcohol.

His mother would be plying him with her homemade tortillas soon enough.

The thought surprised him. He wasn't sure how he felt about seeing her. He had only started calling her in the past ten years because his sister had nagged the hell out of him. Claudia had never understood how he could stay angry, and he didn't get how she'd so easily forgiven Hilda for tearing them away from their father.

The man was dead now. And Ben would never know him. All he had left of his dad were the vague memories of a six-year-old. That, and the bitterness over his mother's betrayal. It still lingered like a hot stone at the edge of a fire. At thirty-three, he was just better at hiding it.

Damn, he wished Claudia was here. She'd always acted as a buffer between him and Hilda. But she was pregnant and couldn't make the trip, so she'd begged and pleaded for him to come.

He'd finally given in last week, not just for Claudia's sake, but for Rachel's, too, and he didn't want to mess things up as a wedding memento. Where was the little firecracker, anyway? He scanned the crowd. How hard was it to find a redheaded bride?

"Oh, my God, Ben, you made it!" Her voice came from behind him.

He turned to find Rachel's green eyes filling with tears.

The last time he'd seen her, she'd just celebrated her twelfth birthday. She'd grown into a beautiful young woman.

She dabbed at her eyes, then picked up her dress and launched herself at him.

He caught her and stumbled back. "Jesus. How many tons of lace are you wearing?" She laughed and hugged him until he set her at arm's length. "Man, you've grown up."

"Hey, watch it. She's taken."

"Matt Gunderson." Ben smiled at her new husband and shook his hand. "Good to see you."

"Yeah, it's been a while." Matt yanked his tie loose with a relieved sigh.

Rachel smacked his wrist. "Stop it. We haven't finished taking pictures."

"Oh, yes, we have."

"Please." Rachel leaned into Matt. "When will I ever get you in a tux again?"

"Never."

"Exactly."

Matt slumped in defeat. "So this is married life, huh?" he muttered while letting Rachel redo his tie. "Stay single, Ben. Do yourself a favor and just stay single."

"Way ahead of you on that one, bro." Ben grinned at Rachel's eye roll.

He liked women. He liked sex even more. Fortunately, he rarely went without. But give a woman that much power over him? Wouldn't happen.

"Have you seen your mom yet?" Rachel asked.

Ben shook his head and looked at Matt. Time to change the subject. "I read somewhere you're going to quit rodeoing."

"I'm done. I rode in Vegas for the last time."

"Why? You were earning big." Ben glanced at Rachel. Would she miss the big prize money, or had she put the screws to him?

Matt shrugged. "I had enough."

"Matt's father died last year and left him the ranch," Rachel said. "So he's running the Lone Wolf and raising rodeo stock."

"*We're* running the Lone Wolf," Matt corrected her, slipping an arm around her.

"Not really. I'm not much help yet. The Sundance guests keep me hopping."

Ben frowned. "Guests?"

"Cole didn't mention it when he saw you in LA," Rachel said with a wry smile. "I'm not surprised. My poor brothers…" She sighed. "We're now part dude ranch."

Ben couldn't have been more shocked. He thought again of the patched roofs and warped wood siding on the barn. The McAllisters had been proud, wealthy cattlemen going back several generations. "Since when?"

"About a year and a half now." She shrugged. "Between the poor economy and drought, all the ranches around here have been suffering. We needed to generate income."

"A dude ranch," Ben murmured. No, he didn't figure Cole would've volunteered that information.

"It was Rachel's idea," Matt said, his tone defensive. "If not for her, they would've had to lay off half the men. Not to mention she had to put her career on hold."

"It's okay, Matt," Rachel said softly. "Ben didn't mean anything. You were just as shocked when you found out, remember?"

"Hey." Ben spread his hands. "I'm surprised, that's all. I'm in the process of buying a ranch myself, out in California. But now you've got me nervous."

Rachel and Matt both frowned. "What, and give up working in Hollywood?" Matt asked. "Dating hot women and walking the red carpet?"

Ben laughed. "Don't believe everything you read on the internet."

Matt inclined his head at Rachel. "It's not my fault. She looks up everybody."

"I do not." She lifted her chin, sending Ben back fifteen years. She'd always been an independent kid. "So you're buying a ranch and giving up stunt work?"

"Eventually. But I'd still be in the business, so to speak. I plan to raise stock that I can supply to films and TV shoots. I'd train the animals, horses in particular, and work with them on the sets. Even commercial ads pay well. In Hollywood, it's all about who you know, and I'm lucky in that department."

"Snag a Super Bowl Ad. That's got to be—" Rachel's gaze shifted to something behind him. "You're about to meet my friend Katy."

"What took her so long?" Matt murmured, then responded to Rachel's stink eye with an innocent look. "What?"

"Be nice," Rachel muttered under her breath and then said to Ben, "I want to hear more later. Hey, Katy."

Ben smiled at the tall, striking brunette who'd joined them, her strapless red dress held up by generous breasts.

"Katy," Rachel said, "this is Ben. I've told you about him. Ben's like another brother to me."

"Yes, I remember." Katy leaned forward to shake his hand, her breasts plumping over the top of the dress, her smile sultry. "I believe you mentioned he wasn't as bad as Trace."

"Thanks." Rachel laughed. "Thanks for that." She looked at Ben. "I meant when I was a kid. You both teased me unmercifully and don't deny it."

Ben forced a smile. His memories weren't quite that benign. "Where is Trace, anyway?" He looked past Katy to do a quick sweep of the crowd, but stopped at a familiar face. Whoa.

Deputy Hendrix had let her hair down in loose waves that skimmed her shoulders. The sunglasses were gone, and she'd traded her uniform for tan slacks and a tailored white blouse that showed off her fit, toned body.

Nice. Very nice.

He wondered if she had her ticket book with her. Maybe after a little champagne, she'd have second thoughts about the one she had written him.

Rachel glanced around, frowning. "I don't see Jesse or Cole, either. They know the photographer wants to take more shots of the wedding party."

"We could go look for them," Katy said, and Ben knew the "we" included him.

He wasn't in the mood for company. Maybe later. "I'll be heading to the house soon," he said. "If I see the guys, I'll send them over. Or drag them out of their rooms if I have to."

"Perfect." Rachel's smile lasted only a second. "Wait. Knock before you go in. Girlfriends may be involved. Or in Cole's case, his wife."

"Cole's married?" He'd never said anything about taking the plunge.

"He and Jamie eloped a month ago to avoid having a big hoopla." She lowered her voice. "Not common knowledge. Just the family knows." She gestured inclusively to Ben. "And now you, too, Katy. But don't say anything."

A group approached to congratulate the newlyweds, and Ben used the opportunity to slip away. He could feel Katy's eyes on his back. He might have played that better, but he'd lost sight of the deputy.

While he searched for her, Ben realized how easy it had been with Rachel and Matt. It felt good that she still considered him family. And so did Cole. As long as Ben did nothing to hurt Hilda. The McAllisters had always been fiercely protective of his mother. Starting with Gavin and Barbara.

Thinking of Gavin McAllister tightened Ben's chest. Missing the man's funeral would haunt him for life. Gavin had treated him like a son right alongside his own boys, never taking sides when they squabbled and disciplining without bias.

Time had a way of lending perspective. Ben understood now that he'd been damn lucky to have Mr. McAllister as a role model.

He looked toward the house, hoping he'd finally catch sight of the deputy, but she wasn't among the people crowding the wide porch. People sat on rockers. Some lounged against the railing. A short, dark-haired woman wound her way through them carrying a large pitcher. He studied her for a moment, taking in the frail stoop of her narrow shoulders. Realization hit him square in the gut.

Mom?

She set down the pitcher and glanced up suddenly, as if she could feel him watching her. He turned, hoping she wouldn't see him.

Something twisted painfully inside his chest, and he had the sudden urge to make a run for the Porsche, drive so fast and far that he'd forget all about the Sundance. Forget about the family who'd given him a home. Forget about the mother who'd never trusted him enough to tell him the truth about his own father.

Hell of a time to figure out he wasn't ready to see her. Certainly not in front of all these people.

Shoving a hand through his hair, he stared at the distant Rockies and the crimson sun sinking behind them. He was struck by the sudden notion that he'd missed more than the mountains. He'd missed the McAllister family. The Sundance. And in spite of her betrayal, his mom.

He hadn't expected this, wasn't prepared to do anything but push the feelings aside. Clear his head.

What he needed was another drink. He'd promised his sister he'd do this thing. Reconnect with their mom. Make some peace. Which felt impossible at the moment.

He found another makeshift bar and was about to pour a scotch when he saw her.

Deputy Hendrix. From the strained curve of her mouth to her stick-straight posture, she seemed uncomfortable. Probably trying to get rid of the old guy in the loud sports jacket who was bending her ear. Ben could help her with that. He smiled, practically seeing her void his ticket.

Before he could approach them, the man walked away. She turned a longing glance toward a row of parked cars, looking as though she wanted to be here as much as Ben did.

Keeping an eye on her, he exchanged the whiskey for a bottle of champagne sitting in an ice bucket and filled two flutes.

GRACE WAS BEGINNING to wish she'd brought her gun. If her uncle didn't stop annoying her, she was pretty sure she could make a case for justifiable homicide. Although since she didn't have a squeaky-clean record, maybe she'd be better off hiding the body. Plenty of good places around here.

Grace swallowed. Dear God. How could she joke about this? Even if only to herself. She was a horrible person. And now she'd lost track of Clarence. He'd disappeared into the crowd. But he'd pop up again and motion for her to meet yet another person who simply wanted to enjoy the party and not be bullied by the mayor.

Maybe she should make a run for her car. Now. While she had the chance. She hated that Rachel might see her, but Grace could always apologize later and pretend she'd been ill.

"Well, don't you clean up nicely."

The deep voice sent a flutter down her spine. Taking a moment to compose herself, she met his eyes. "I'm not tearing up the ticket."

Ben just smiled and passed her a flute. "I'd planned to

rescue you a minute ago. I figured that might soften you up, but I was too late."

"Rescue me?"

He glanced back at the crowd. "I saw some guy bothering you."

"Who?"

"An old guy with a bad comb-over."

Grace laughed. Oh, wouldn't Clarence love to hear that description. "Better watch it. He's the mayor."

"Figures."

"And my uncle."

"Ah. My apologies." With that lazy smile of his, he looked about as apologetic as a tomcat toying with a mouse. No, he didn't care who Clarence was to her or the town. "I didn't want him chasing you off before we could get better acquainted."

Grace snorted a laugh. He was smooth, a real charmer. In her line of work, she met quite a few, usually trying to talk their way out of an arrest.

"You don't believe me?" He was watching her, studying her face with a faintly bemused expression that she didn't care for. Though fair was fair. She'd given him the once-over earlier. The difference was, while she'd admired his bronzed skin, he was probably counting her freckles.

She stared at the champagne she'd absently accepted from him. "I really shouldn't drink this," she said and took a sip. "I have to drive."

"You can't have far to go. Not in this town."

She moved slightly so his shoulder blocked the remaining rays of sunlight and she didn't have to squint at him. He had a strong jaw, a symmetrical face. "Most accidents happen within five miles of home."

Amusement brought out the gold flecks in his eyes. "Makes sense. Statistically speaking." He paused. "Are you going to tell me your first name?"

"You can call me deputy."

He seemed momentarily startled, then threw his head back and laughed. So loudly that people turned and stared. Including Chloe and the other blond bridesmaid standing by the tent pole. Grace got the feeling they'd been watching her and Ben all along. They were probably wondering why he'd approached her. Grace wondered the same thing.

She cleared her throat. "It's Grace."

"Grace," he repeated, and surprised her by offering his hand.

His palm was rough against hers, which wasn't exactly soft and tender, either. "It's a pleasure to meet you, Grace. The name suits you."

"Um…really not so much."

Ben's brows lifted, just a tiny bit, as though she intrigued him. He'd be disappointed. If only she'd left when she had the chance.

After studying her a moment, his attention drifted toward the house. He watched the guests gathered on the porch and then swept a gaze over the tent crowd. Most likely plotting an escape.

"Lucky it didn't rain today," she murmured, searching the sky. A few clouds hovered but none threatened. "I heard Rachel pushed the date back, hoping for an outdoor wedding."

He said nothing, but she sensed his amusement at her feeble attempt to change the subject. She saw a band setting up on the stage and realized the oak planks in front of it served as a dance floor. No way she'd stick around for dancing. It would be just like Clarence to drag her up there with some cowboy. Not Ben, though. She imagined her uncle would give him a wide berth.

Katy had joined her friends and they all were staring at Grace and Ben. The brunette looked sulky and Grace wondered what had happened between her and Ben.

"Beautiful, aren't they?" Ben murmured.

Grace blinked. Talk about rude and unexpected. Not that he'd get a rise out of her. "They're Rachel's sorority sisters," she said, turning back to him.

He frowned. "Who?"

"The bridesmaids. Rachel's friends."

He followed her gaze, his frown deepening. With a short laugh, he looked at Grace. "I was referring to the Rockies."

"Oh." She silently cursed herself and her fair skin, then gave the mountains her complete attention. "Yes, they are breathtaking."

"That snow melts and comes streaming all the way to the foothills," he said, pointing. "Four-wheelers can make it clear to that ridge when it's not too muddy. People go up just to see the wildflowers."

She squinted, trying to follow the direction of his finger. "Why am I not seeing a ridge?"

"Come here." He took her arm and stationed her in front of him. Placing a hand on her shoulder, he ducked down to her eye level, his cheek close to hers. "Right there," he said, gesturing with the champagne flute. "See where the aspens are still bare?"

She nodded, the movement causing her cheek to rub against his stubbled jaw. Her skin tingled. Not just at the point of contact, either, but all the way down her back.

Grace didn't like it. Didn't like that she could so acutely feel the heat from his body. Hated that his touch had awoken a sudden yearning. She didn't need the aggravation of wanting something she couldn't have.

She swallowed. "That's pretty high up for a quad to go," she said, moving her shoulder and shifting to the side.

"You can't be squeamish. On some of those trails, your tires are hugging the edge." Ben finally lowered his hand. "It's not as bad as it sounds. You tip over and sure, you'll get beat up some, but you won't slide all the way down. Eventually the trees will stop your fall."

That made her laugh. "So, you could break your arms and legs, and God knows what else. And likely total your four-wheeler. Explain to me how that's not so bad."

His smile alone would make any sane woman run and hide. "Hell, if you put it that way…"

"I heard you're a stunt man, so your perspective might be skewed."

He shrugged. "Kids go up there all the time. Back in high school, Cole, Jesse, along with half the football team, we all used to go up there. We survived."

She sighed. "I miss those days. Being certain I knew *everything* was so comforting."

Eyes narrowed, Ben searched her face, giving her the feeling he'd taken her casual remark personally. "You're not from the area," he said finally.

"I moved here two weeks ago." She paused when she heard someone call his name. "I think you're being summoned." She nodded toward the tent.

Ben turned. "Is that Trace?"

"I believe so." She hadn't actually met the youngest McAllister brother, but no mistaking the resemblance to Cole and Jesse.

"Jesus. He was thirteen when I left. Tall and skinny as a rail." Ben lifted his hand in acknowledgment, the fondness in his gaze kind of sweet. "The kid talked horses and trucks nonstop. And girls. He was worried his brothers and I weren't going to leave him any."

"Did you?"

His slow smile was ridiculously sexy. "A few."

"They're motioning for you to join them. Go ahead. I think they're taking pictures."

"Come with me."

"No." Grace shook her head, surprised he'd asked. "They're your family. I'd feel awkward."

He hesitated as if he wanted to argue the point, but then just nodded. "Don't go anywhere. Okay?"

She simply smiled. She never made a promise she couldn't keep.

3

BEN WASN'T IN a hurry to reach the group. He scanned the people surrounding Rachel and Matt, not keen on unexpectedly coming face-to-face with his mother. He'd see her soon, but not with everyone watching.

"Get over here, Carter." Trace held a pair of longnecks in one hand and motioned with the other.

Ben hadn't gone by Carter for a long time. His last name was Wolf now and had been for thirteen years, since he'd scraped together enough money to legally change it. Carter had never been his real name, anyway. Nor Hilda's. She'd made it up after she'd run out on his father, whose name she refused to divulge.

Jesse was standing beside Trace. Cole was there, too, along with a couple of women Ben didn't recognize. Rachel was trying in vain to get everyone's attention while an older man set up a camera.

"Rachel got you in a tux, huh?" Ben extended his hand to Trace, who ignored it and gave him a hearty one-armed hug.

"Man, it's good to see you," Trace said, his voice deeper now.

"Yeah, it's been a while," Ben said casually, unprepared for the emotion washing over him. He'd been fairly tight with Cole and Jesse. They were close in age and shared many of the same interests. But with Trace, the bond was different.

He'd been a baby when Ben moved to the Sundance. Trace had grown up thinking of Ben as his older brother, often confiding in him instead of Cole or Jesse. The day Ben had told him he was leaving, Trace had punched a door and broken his hand.

Cole and Jesse joined them, only briefly. After the hand-shaking was done, the photographer asked them to move a few tables.

Trace left the task to his older brothers and nodded at Ben's empty flute. "You don't have to drink that champagne crap. Here." With a grin, Trace offered him a long-neck. "We saved the good stuff for immediate family."

Ben accepted the beer, saw Trace's jeans and cowboy boots, and laughed.

Trace tugged at the lapel of his tux jacket. "Rachel hasn't noticed yet." He looked guiltily over his shoulder. "I didn't know she wanted more pictures so I went inside and changed. As long as that photographer dude shoots from the waist up, it shouldn't matter."

Ben shook his head. "She's gonna kick your ass."

"I know. If she doesn't, Nikki will."

"Your girlfriend?"

Trace shrugged. "In three months, we'll be getting hitched, too, so she's a little more than that, I guess."

"Ya think?" Ben's laughter turned a few heads.

"Nice. Get me in trouble," Trace said, glancing around. "By the way, the Porsche...yours or a rental?"

"I bought it last year and got ticketed twice in three weeks."

"Only twice?" Trace took a pull of his beer. "You gonna let me take it for a spin?"

"You finally learn how to use a clutch?"

Ben waited for Trace to remember the driving lessons.

Teaching a twelve-year-old to drive hadn't been one of his wiser ideas.

Trace winced. "Ah, man, that was humiliating."

The second time he'd gotten behind the wheel of the ranch's old Ford, Trace had clipped a tree and smashed the side mirror. Ben had taken the blame rather than admit his stupidity.

"You still owe me," he said. "Your dad made me pay for the repair out of my salary."

"Yep, I do. I'll even tack on interest."

Ben smiled. "I had no business letting you drive." He flashed back to another day, another time, and took a gulp of beer. "I didn't know about your dad," he said quietly. "About the cancer, or that he'd passed away. I found out much later."

"I know." Trace clapped him on the back. "Everyone knew you would've come back if you'd heard in time."

"My fault for not keeping in touch." Ben surprised himself with the admission. He'd always felt his mom was to blame for everything that was wrong in his life. Her claim that she'd run from abuse didn't completely add up. Why isolate herself and her kids from her own family? Ben didn't know his grandparents. Or where he was born. Or if he had uncles, aunts and cousins.

It was one thing to lie to a couple of kids, but once they'd turned eighteen, he and Claudia had a right to know, even if the truth was messy. Hilda's silence was a barrier he'd never been able to cross. The longer his mother continued to lie to them, the more convinced Ben became that she was hiding the truth not just about their father, but also about herself. Why else would she keep her silence? The man was dead.

"Ben?" Trace's tone indicated it wasn't the first time he'd tried to get Ben's attention. "Rachel wants us. The photographer's waiting."

"She wants you, not me."

"Wanna bet?"

"Benedicto," Rachel's voice carried over the murmurs of the bridal party who'd gathered near the stage. "Get over here."

"See?" Trace grumbled. "Still bossy as hell."

Ben had to smile. He gave Rachel a small shake of his head, and her glare turned pleading.

"For what it's worth, your mom's busy in the kitchen," Trace said quietly, then strolled toward the waiting group.

Ben glanced at Katy and the other bridesmaids eyeing him as if he were a juicy steak. Normally, he'd already have decided on his companion for later. But he was restless, edgy.

And there was Grace to consider. Something about her quiet beauty and wit appealed to him. Add the fact that she was a refreshing challenge. She hadn't flirted with him once. He turned to see if he should pick up another drink for her. She could probably tempt him into...

She wasn't where he had left her.

He looked toward the house, then panned across a group of women huddled near the bar. Grace wasn't among them. He could tell they were local women, though none he recognized. A pair of older cowboys carrying guitars emerged from a row of parked trucks.

Ben squinted at a blur of movement behind them and caught a glimpse of her. Only for a second. He waited a moment, watching to see if maybe she'd gone to get something out of her car. A minute later, a silver compact drove out the driveway.

Disappointment settled like a weight on his shoulders. He shrugged it off. Now wasn't the time for a hookup, anyway. Especially not with the local law. He had too much crap swirling in his head. He craned his neck for a look at the Porsche. He'd parked it between the stable and a tree, where another vehicle couldn't fit. He didn't need his doors getting dinged.

Arriving late had been by design. He'd wanted everyone to see him driving the Porsche, prove to them he wasn't a charity case. Yet he'd forgotten all about the damn thing until Trace had mentioned it.

Ben drew air deep into his lungs. Nothing was going the way he'd expected. And he'd prepared for plenty...anger, resentment, even nerves.

But shit.

He'd never expected to feel like he'd come home.

GRACE GRABBED KEYS out of her desk drawer and holstered her gun. She didn't have to look at Danny and Roy to know they were smirking like a couple of jackasses. They did every time she brought out her Glock, as if they'd never seen a woman carry a gun before. Scary to think those two were actually deputies.

"So, how did you enjoy the party last night?" Roy asked, leaning back in his chair, his fingers locked behind his head, his round belly straining his uniform shirt.

She'd been waiting for him to mention the reception. Just to cause trouble. "It was great."

"You left early."

Grace raised her brows. "I hope your wife didn't notice you were keeping track of me. She might get the wrong idea."

Danny chuckled, and Roy shot him a dirty look.

"Tell me something, Grace," Roy said, "why do you suppose that you, being a newcomer and all, got an invite to the wedding and Danny, Wade and Gus didn't?"

Of course this was about her being the mayor's niece. "I guess you'll have to ask Rachel or Matt that question." She set her blue ball cap on her head.

"Quit wearing that stupid thing. Get yourself a Stetson so you look like a real deputy," Danny said and abruptly swung his boots off the desk.

"Oh, I should emulate you two so I can fit in?" She

turned for the door, muttering under her breath, "Maybe if I lost fifty IQ points."

Noah was standing in the open doorway, not six feet away.

That's why Danny had snapped to attention—

Oh, God. "Hi, boss," she said, her cheeks burning. Of course Noah had heard her. She'd apologize for the unprofessional remark later. But damned if she'd do it in front of Roy and Danny.

At least the sheriff didn't look annoyed. In fact, he seemed to be controlling a smile. She liked Noah. An ex-Chicago police detective, he was sharp, professional and moving on to work for the marshal service.

"I thought you were off today, Noah," Roy said, remaining relaxed in his chair, exercising his familiarity with their boss for Grace's benefit.

"I just came by to get something." Noah stopped and eyed Roy. "Do me a favor."

"Name it."

"Order another uniform shirt."

"But, boss—"

"I don't want to hear it." Shaking his head, Noah walked to his desk. "We've had this discussion twice already."

Roy moved his hands from behind his head and glared at Grace. So now she was to blame for him blowing his diet?

"Who's on patrol?" Noah asked.

"I am." She paused with her hand on the doorknob. "I was just headed out. Need something?"

"Take a few traffic cones with you in case you run into any mudslides. The rain came down fairly hard around midnight."

Grace nodded, making a mental note to jot down the information. She'd started a notebook to record all the little things the other deputies already knew from growing up here. The doorknob shook. Someone outside was trying to open the door, so she pulled her hand back.

It was Clarence. Oh, great.

"Good morning, Mayor," she said and stepped aside.

He crossed the threshold, his sour expression changing the instant he noticed the men. "Mornin' Sheriff Calder, deputies," he said, nodding at them. He stopped in front of Roy. "Don't we have money in the budget for uniforms? Get yourself a bigger size, son, before you pop a button and take out someone's eye."

Roy's face turned red. He straightened, sucking in his gut.

Grace sighed. Clarence was a politician. How could he not understand diplomacy? And how on earth had he stayed in office for so long?

"What can I do for you, Mayor?" Noah pulled a folder out of his desk drawer.

"Actually, I stopped by to see Grace." Clarence turned to look her up and down, frowning first at her jeans, then at her cap. "Where are you off to?"

"I'm on duty."

"We should discuss a proper uniform for the department. Maybe tan slacks to match the shirt," he said, glancing at Noah. "What do you think?"

"Waste of money. Peace officers in this county have been wearing jeans as far back as I can remember. The shirt's enough."

"Just because something's always been done a certain way doesn't make it right," Clarence said, his tone querulous.

Noah smiled. "No, but tan slacks aren't going to help the public identify the sheriff or deputies. Anyway, not my call. Hash it out with the new sheriff."

Clarence grunted. "What do you think, Grace?"

At first, she was speechless. She refused to look at Roy

or Danny. "Sheriff Calder is right. Whoever replaces him should help make that decision."

Her uncle's gaze narrowed. "I'll walk you out. I need to have a word with you."

Nodding, she briefly met Noah's sympathetic eyes. He was a good sheriff, a good man. Filling his shoes wouldn't be easy.

"You left the party early," Clarence said once they were on the sidewalk. His face lit up at the sight of a blonde middle-aged woman walking toward them. He passed a hand over the sparse strands of auburn hair slicked across his pink scalp.

"I wasn't feeling well." It wasn't a complete lie. Between him and Ben, she'd felt a bit off.

"Morning, Laura." Clarence and the woman exchanged smiles as she passed.

"Do you know where the traffic cones are stored?"

He snapped his attention back to Grace. "How would I know? Don't try and change the subject."

"What subject?" She remembered the storage closet behind the office and studied her set of keys. "That I left early? So what?"

"Not that. I want to know about Ben. Hilda's boy."

Grace glanced up. "What about him?"

"It seemed you two had a lot to talk about." Clarence's small, shrewd eyes searched her face.

She hurried her pace in case she blushed. "Yup, the McAllisters and the weather. It was a fascinating discussion."

"Don't you sass me, young lady."

"Mayor Leland, I'm on duty. I am working." She turned left down the narrow alley.

"Where are we going?"

"The storage closet behind the office."

"Why did we have to come this way? We could've used the back door."

She preferred that he hadn't followed at all. Ignoring him, she located the correct key, found the cones and carried them to the truck. Of course, Clarence stayed on her heels. She opened the driver's door.

"You hold on a minute," he said. "I know that boy, and what I have to say is for your own good. You should appreciate I'm looking out for you."

Grace wanted to tell her uncle that whatever it was had to wait until she clocked out. But she couldn't stand waiting all day. "Okay, what is it?"

"His mother, Hilda, is a good, God-fearing woman. She raised a fine daughter, and I'm sure she tried with Ben." Clarence shook his head. "He was just one of those kids who couldn't seem to keep his nose clean. The minute he entered his teens, he was nothing but trouble."

"What kind of trouble? What did he do?"

Clarence seemed surprised by the question. "Now, you don't need to be concerned with details," he said, his condescending tone suggesting *she shouldn't worry her pretty little head.* "Just take my word for it. You steer clear of him before he tarnishes your reputation."

Grace smiled. Her uncle had no idea what he was talking about. He'd probably heard some rumors or knew Ben hadn't seen his mom in some time, which made him plain bad to the bone.

"You know I'm telling you this for your own good, don't you, Gracie?"

"Well, while we're on the subject," she said sweetly, "I'll remind you again that singling me out in front of the other deputies is not helpful. They already resent me."

"Oh, for heaven's sake, this isn't the city. We all know each other around here. You and I are related. So what?"

She forced a smile. "Have a nice day, Mayor," she said and climbed into the truck.

Fortunately, he spotted a couple of his constituents and glided along the sidewalk to shake hands, letting her go without an argument. Good. The election was months away, but the more he campaigned to get reelected, the less he would bother her.

After an hour of driving around checking for mudslides, Grace pulled over and opened her thermos. She'd left a few orange cones at the base of a popular hiking trail, but that was it. Everything looked okay.

One thing Montana had over Arizona was rain. And lots of it. She'd been leaving her window open at night. The inn where she was staying was located on Main Street, and a couple times she'd heard noise coming from the bar several blocks down. But it was worth it just to hear the patter of rain on the windowsill.

She sipped her coffee, anxious for the much-needed caffeine to give her a boost. Kind of a shame, really. The peace and quiet made her pleasantly mellow. She glanced into the rearview mirror. Nothing but blacktop, blue sky and woods for miles.

What the—?

She stared at the red blur until she could make out the shape of the Porsche. The car hugged the curve of the road, then raced toward her. Was he out of his mind?

Ben had been right. She didn't have radar, but she'd bet anything he was going well over the fifty-mile speed limit. Grace started the engine and hit the flashing lights just as the car came up on her. The vehicle whizzed past.

She hesitated, torn between anger at his recklessness and a reluctance to give him another ticket. Depending on his record, it could cost him his license. But then, maybe it should. Maybe this was the lesson he needed. Either way, this was her job.

Hastily getting the truck on the road, she cursed at the spilled coffee wetting her jeans. She pushed the accelerator all the way to the floor. The older model truck didn't have a chance of catching up to the Porsche. So it surprised her when Ben slowed and coasted until she came up behind him.

She glimpsed his dark hair as he pulled onto the shoulder, and she felt a little sadness that her uncle might be right about Ben. Mostly, though, she was mad.

Breathing deeply, she grabbed her ticket book and pen, then climbed out of the truck. She kept her sunglasses on, unwilling to let him see her anger and disappointment. Did he think he could charm her out of another ticket?

"This seems all too familiar," she said as the tinted window lowered. "License and—" She blinked. "Trace?"

"Mornin', Deputy," he said with a sheepish grin.

"I thought you were Ben." She cleared her throat, annoyed at the surge of relief she felt. "Do you know how fast you were going?"

"Too fast." He shoved a hand through his hair. "You're going to ticket me. I know and I deserve it. But so you don't think I'm a total idiot, I cut loose for only a couple miles to see what the Porsche could do." He reached into his back pocket. "I don't usually speed, not in my truck." His mouth curved in a boyish grin. "Not by much anyway."

Grace watched him slide his license out of his wallet. She sighed. "I'll give you a verbal warning," she said, lowering the ticket book to her side.

Trace's face lit up, and he was quick to make his license disappear. "Thanks. I mean it. You won't catch me speeding again."

"Good. Because next time, no mercy. Not even at five miles over."

His expression fell. "Five," he repeated. "Huh."

Hiding her smile, she headed back to the truck, wondering if she dared analyze why she was so pleased the driver hadn't been Ben.

4

THE TENT WAS GONE, along with the tables and chairs. Ben shouldn't have been surprised. People in the country woke early and went right to work. He'd been one of them once.

He stood near the stable waiting for Trace to bring back the Porsche. In the bright sunlight, the Sundance looked even more run-down than it had last night. The place wasn't an eyesore, nothing like that. In fact, their paying guests might consider the buildings quaint and rustic. And for all he knew, that was the point of not keeping things pristine. But he doubted it. The McAllisters had too much pride.

A dude ranch…

Ben still couldn't believe it. Gavin McAllister must be turning over in his grave. He'd been a cattleman to the bone, and proud of it. But he'd been a husband and father first, and willing to do anything to take care of his own. And that had once included Ben.

Blocking the sun with his hand, he squinted down the gravel driveway. Trace had been gone awhile now. What the hell…was he halfway to Kalispell? Maybe Ben should've warned him about Grace. The other deputies wouldn't ticket him. To some extent, Ben understood why she had to be a hard-ass. Still, she could've given him a warning.

He glanced at his watch and shook his head in amazement. Trace had been gone only seven minutes. Hardly long enough to get the Porsche revved.

No mystery what had Ben edgy. He turned to the house, wondering if Hilda was standing at a window, watching him. The chaos in the kitchen had kept him from seeing her last night. Okay, fine. Nothing would have stopped him if he'd truly wanted to see her. His sister had slung the accusation after waking him with an early call. Claudia hadn't tried his cell phone. No, she'd rung the inn and asked someone to pound on his door at 8:00 a.m. when she knew he'd still be sleeping. Probably to punish him for not staying at the Sundance.

Claudia refused to understand he couldn't just waltz in after a fifteen-year absence. Hilda would want to know everything that had happened to him. He'd never admit he'd had it rough in LA after leaving the Sundance. A big olive-skinned kid like him who fit a nice, neat stereotype of a freeloading illegal brought a lot of unwanted attention. For months, he'd been stopped, questioned and frisked almost daily. Sometimes the shakedowns had been warranted, most times not. So no, he wasn't overly fond of law enforcement in any form.

It had shocked him to learn Noah Calder was sheriff of Blackfoot Falls. When they'd been kids, Noah had practically lived at the Sundance, getting into his share of trouble right alongside Ben.

Maybe he should stop by the office when he got back to town. And just maybe he'd see Grace.

Giving in to the inevitable, he started toward the house. Distracted by thoughts of Grace's pale, creamy skin, he almost didn't see Cole walking out of the stable.

"Hey, Ben." He pulled off his work gloves. "I didn't

know you were here. Find me before you leave. I want to
show you something."

Ben veered his way. "What's that?"

"It can wait," Cole said, glancing at the house.

"We're here now."

Cole smiled. "Okay. Come on. It won't take long."

As they entered the stable Ben breathed in the familiar
scents of saddle soap and leather. He was glad to see the
tack wall was in primo condition.

They passed five stalls before Cole stopped and motioned with his chin. "Look familiar?"

Ben stared at the long-legged colt, noticed the identify-
ing snip of white between the nostrils. "Is Zorro the sire?"

"Yep." Standing with his arms folded, his feet planted
wide, Cole looked on like a proud papa. "This is Milo."

"How old?"

"Four and half months. Just been weaned."

"You gonna sell him?"

"Nope. He's staying right here."

"You ever change your mind, call me."

Cole looked over at him. "So you're going through with
it. You're buying that ranch?"

Ben had forgotten he'd mentioned it to him in LA. "As
soon as I get back to California and sign the papers."

"Good for you, bro. You should be working with horses.
Dad always said he'd never seen anyone better with an
Arabian than you."

Ben's chest tightened. He didn't remember that, but he
believed Cole. "You been doing much breeding?"

He shrugged. "Not really. Why?"

"I'll be in the market for stock soon." Ben hadn't considered the possibility before now, but he liked the idea of
being able to give them some business.

"You must have closer ranches and auctions," Cole said,
the interest in his eyes at odds with his nonchalant words.

"I'll need startup stock with good lineage, a few smart,

trainable horses. If you decide to breed, we'd be talking more about stud services. I may do some breeding myself later on, but for now I'm more interested in doing the training. Bottom line? Whatever we work out, I trust you. You wouldn't believe what a rare commodity that is in Hollywood."

Cole rubbed his jaw, squinting at the colt while he thought. "Sure. You know Trace…he's always been more interested in horses than the cattle. He'd be all over a breeding program."

Cole's cell rang. He was needed in the east barn, so Ben walked out with him. They agreed to talk more before he left for LA, and then Ben headed toward the house.

He'd barely knocked once when Barbara McAllister flung the door wide. "Ben. Oh, my goodness, you're even taller than when you left," she said, and pulled him into a hug. "I'm glad you came."

Ben smiled. She was so tiny that her arms couldn't reach all the way around him. "You look good, Mrs. McAllister. How are you?"

"I'm fine." She leaned back. "Look at you, so handsome. I saw you last night from the porch, but with all those people here, I couldn't get to you before you disappeared."

"I knew you all were busy, so I stayed away from the house. I figured today would be better."

"Well, your mom is very anxious to see you. How about we go to the kitchen? I bet you still know the way. It was always your favorite room in the house."

"Mrs. McAllister, are you implying I ate like a horse?"

"Of course not. None of you boys did." She rolled her eyes. "You're an adult now. Call me Barbara so I don't feel like I'm a hundred and ten."

"Come on now, Barbara, you know you could be Rachel's twin."

With a laugh, she wagged a finger at him. "You," she said, "are too charming for your own good."

She had to be in her midfifties, but she still looked youthful, her skin smooth and unlined except for the laugh lines around her eyes. He was about to follow her then realized something was different about the house. Sunlight shining in through a two-story window flooded the foyer and living room.

"That's new," he said, amazed he hadn't noticed last night.

"It was Cole's winter project a few years ago. Before—" She sighed. "Before things got a bit tight around here. I don't mean only the Sundance. The whole community has suffered."

Jesus, he hadn't considered how the poor economy had affected small rural towns. The film business had felt the pinch also, though obviously not like the rest of the country. Made him more eager to do business with the McAllisters.

At the door shared by the dining room and the kitchen, Barbara stopped and lowered her voice. "I'll let you go in by yourself."

"No, you don't have to—"

"Yes." She gave him a gentle smile and squeezed his hand. "I do. We're all so glad you're here," she said and slipped away.

Ben inhaled deeply. Feminine laughter wafted from the back of the house. It would be so easy to find a distraction. Postpone seeing Hilda for another day. He didn't have to be back in LA until the loan was finalized. In just over a week, the Ventura ranch would be all his. Well, his and Lena's, but she was a silent partner, a venture capitalist with one foot in the film business. She had her hands in a variety of projects and knew nothing about ranching or horses. Turning a profit was all she cared about.

It was eerily quiet on the other side of the door. Normally, he'd hear pots banging around, Hilda humming. The woman loved to hum or sing. It didn't matter what kind of music or in what language. She was probably wringing her hands, waiting for him to come through the door.

Might as well get it over with. He pushed the door open. She sat at the oak table, her hands clasped tightly together.

"Benedicto," she murmured, her voice catching as she got to her feet. "I can't believe you're really here. You're a man now. Tall and handsome."

Wrinkles lined her face. Her eyes looked tired. Partly because of him, he imagined. And partly because of the lies she'd been unable to keep straight over the years. All variations on a theme. Why his father never came to see them. Why they'd left the house he and Claudia had loved. Why they had no grandparents or cousins. And finally, that his father was dead. Regardless of the cause, her dark brown eyes were filled with sadness, and his chest tightened in unexpected sympathy.

"Hello, Mom." He went to her and she opened her arms to him. A tear slipped down her cheek just before he hugged her. Some of the resentment that had weighed him down lifted as memories—good ones—from his early childhood rushed through his mind.

All was not forgiven, though. He still had questions, and if she thought him being here absolved her of the lies and deceit, she was wrong.

When she finally released him, Ben expected her to lead him to the table so the long overdue talk could begin. But after she ran a hand down his chest, she went straight to the fridge.

Ben sighed. She would fill him with a homemade meal, tell him…whatever, and barely look at him again. At least he recognized the ground rules: she wouldn't tell the truth and he wouldn't confront her. The relief was instantaneous. He was off the hook for now. And so was she. But he wasn't leaving Montana without knowing exactly what happened with his father.

GRACE SENSED SOMEONE standing behind her and turned to
see Roy looking over her shoulder as she finished her end-
of-shift report. "Yes? Did you want something?"

"Give out any more tickets today?" Roy chuckled.
"Can't believe you cited Ben. I bet that pissed him off
real good."

"Not my problem." She shuffled some papers and ob-
scured Roy's view. "He shouldn't have been speeding."

"That hard-ass attitude ain't gonna win you any friends
around here."

A sarcastic remark almost slipped out. But that would be
stupid. Curious, she asked, "So, you wouldn't have given
him a ticket?"

Roy walked over to the coffeemaker sitting on a metal
filing cabinet. Only the two of them were in the office.
Danny was out on patrol, and it was Wade's day off. And
Gus, he worked a couple days a week. She'd never heard
of a part-time deputy position before.

Roy's eyebrows drew together as he refilled his mug.
He'd never impressed her as someone who thought before speaking.

"It's not a trick question, Roy. I'm honestly just curious."

He studied her for a moment, then dumped a ton of
sugar into his coffee. "I doubt it," he said finally.

"Does anyone ever give speeding tickets?"

"Sure." He shrugged. "Out on the highway. But here?
Not too often. Usually it's the high school kids we stop.
Or tourists."

"Thank you." She smiled at him. "That's good to know."

"No problem." Frowning, he concentrated on stirring
his coffee.

She wanted to tell him not to worry. He wasn't consort-
ing with the enemy. She was merely another deputy trying
to do her job. And contrary to popular belief, whoever was

named acting sheriff wasn't guaranteed a permanent position. The November election would settle that.

In the meantime, they didn't have to be friends, but it would be nice to have a tension-free work environment. Roy could be decent at times, Danny was a follower, but Wade was a problem. The self-appointed ringleader had quit the department months ago and then returned thinking he'd slide right into the vacant sheriff's position. Roy wanted the job, too, but when it came down to it, he was no match for Wade.

According to Clarence, Noah didn't think either man was qualified. But knowing her uncle as she was beginning to, she'd be wise to believe only half of what he told her.

Roy sipped from his chipped blue mug, staring at her over the rim. "You think you're gonna like it here?"

"Honestly, I don't know. It's very different from where I grew up."

"I've been to Texas once," he said. "But not Arizona."

"Well, this is the first time I've been this far north. It's pretty country, though I'm not too anxious to drive in snow."

"Ah, you'll get used to it. We keep the roads clear." Roy sat down, which delighted her.

They were both officially off duty. He usually left the moment he finished his report. Instead, they were having a civilized conversation.

"You lived in Tucson, right?"

"No, about eighty miles west of the city. I grew up in a fairly small town. Maybe twice the size of Blackfoot Falls." Her father had been the sheriff there for thirty-two years before he had retired. Just as her grandfather had held the office before him. It hurt to think she would never carry the torch.

"Were you close to the Mexican border where they have all those drug problems?"

"Close enough to keep us on our toes." She hoped he

didn't pursue the subject of drugs or anything that would lead to questions about her last job.

"See, I'd take snow over chasing drug dealers or cartel honchos any day," he said with a grin.

Grace relaxed. "You have an excellent point."

"Now, I heard you were part of a joint task force with the DEA and Tucson PD. Is that right?"

Her heart sank. Being as truthful as possible was her best bet. "Briefly," she said, wondering if she was being set up. Had Roy pretended to befriend her to dig for dirt? Or was he just curious? "When the cartels switched routes to ship the drugs north, some of the outlying counties were forced to become involved. We were one of the lucky winners."

Roy frowned, shaking his head. "That's rough. I mean, you don't sign up for that horse pucky, and all of a sudden, it's on your doorstep. Bet you were glad to leave that crap behind."

Grace smiled. There was no cunning plot to uncover her past. The guy was simply trying to make conversation.

Her cell rang. She saw it was Clarence and hesitated, not sure she wanted to answer. Though he'd find her eventually.

The second she said, "Hello, Mayor, what can I do for you?" she realized she'd made a face, and that Roy had seen it.

THE WATERING HOLE was crowded for a Sunday evening, every wobbly table and mismatched chair taken. Grace suspected Rachel's friends had something to do with the abundance of cowboys sidled up to the old mahogany bar or playing pool in the back room. Katy and the other two bridesmaids were there. So was another woman Grace recognized from the party. The four of them were having a fine time flirting and dancing.

Grace felt badly for occupying a table for forty minutes.

But she'd stupidly expected Clarence to show up at 6:30 p.m. like he'd promised. Meeting here hadn't even been her idea. He'd claimed he wanted her to meet a couple of his friends and, trying to be cordial, she agreed.

Now she was thinking it might've been a ploy to force her to get out and mingle with the townsfolk. She had no problem with that since she wanted to get to know people. But in her own good time. In fact, she'd visited The Watering Hole twice already. The drinks were cheap, the people friendly, the decor quaint, but of course, the atmosphere was nothing like the neighborhood bar she'd frequented with her cop buddies in Tucson. The reminder that her life had changed forever depressed her.

On the upside, she liked Sadie, the older woman who owned the place. Most of the area's hired hands dropped by at some point during the week, and they all knew better than to break one of her rules. It was awesome how she'd get a rabble-rouser to tuck his tail with just a single look.

Grace returned the smile of a good-looking blond cowboy sitting two tables down, eyeing her. If it turned out he couldn't tell the difference between a friendly smile and a flirty one, she wasn't worried. He'd cool off the moment he found out she was the new deputy. It had worked like a charm so far.

Taking a sip of her now-warm beer, she waited impatiently for Nikki to deliver pitchers to the pool players. Grace wanted to catch her so she could pay her tab and take off.

The door opened and she glanced over, hoping it wasn't her uncle. Ben strolled in, pausing, his gaze sweeping the bar. Grace looked down and took another gulp of the disgusting beer. She'd be foolish to think he wouldn't see her. Even so, he'd most likely ignore her. She'd done something very stupid…stopping Trace and not giving him a ticket… Ben had to have heard…

"It's Ben!"

Rachel's friends had perked up. Good. They wouldn't leave him alone for long.

Chancing a peek, Grace watched Ben head straight to the bar. He spoke with Sadie, his back to everyone. Damn, but the man knew how to wear a pair of jeans. The denim hugged his long legs and butt as though they might've been tailored for him. Even the plain black T-shirt stretching across his broad shoulders seemed anything but ordinary.

She wondered if he'd ever wanted to act instead of do someone else's stunts. He certainly had the looks. But he'd also need the acting chops.

Digging into her pocket for money, she found lip balm and her room key. She tried the other pocket, deciding she needed to get more organized or start carrying a purse. Like that would happen. Finally she pulled out some bills and found a ten.

"Excuse me, ma'am."

She looked up.

It was the blond guy who'd been watching her. He smiled and touched the brim of his hat. "If you aren't expecting anyone, I'd sure like to join you."

"The lady's waiting for me." Ben set a frosty mug in front of her, his steady gaze and faint smile daring her to contradict him.

Her mouth opened, but she couldn't think of anything fast enough.

The cowboy nodded at Ben, then returned to his table. Ben pulled out the chair across from her and sat down with his beer.

She raised her brows at him. "What makes you think I'm not expecting someone?"

"Sadie said you've been sitting here for quite a while."

Figures. Grace looked toward the back. Nikki was taking forever. "Actually, I was just leaving."

"You can't have one beer with me?"

At his brusque tone, Grace stiffened. "Sure," she said

and met his detached gaze. She had the feeling her earlier error in judgment was about to take a bite out of her. Not that she had to explain herself to him. Damned if she'd do that.

5

BEN HAD SWORN he'd keep his cool when he saw Grace again. But he hadn't expected it to be this soon after his visit with his mother. The whole time he'd been at the Sundance with her, she'd been doing something for someone. Filling a thermos, making sandwiches, keeping the floor swept. She never forgot she was the McAllisters' maid even as she asked him questions, while avoiding his with a laugh or a wave of her hand. It made him want to run and never turn back.

And now he was looking at another reminder of where he was in the pecking order. Grace was already friends with the McAllisters and probably hadn't said two words to his mom.

Okay, maybe Grace was different, but he wouldn't bet on it. Already she was giving the family preferential treatment.

Still, she looked great in a plain button-down red shirt and jeans, though he wished she'd left her hair down.

He wondered who'd stood her up. "I heard you stopped Trace."

"I did." She took an unhurried sip of beer. "Thanks for this, by the way."

"My pleasure." He kept his voice even and waited for

her to offer an explanation. Obviously, it wasn't going to happen. "I'm curious about something..."

"What's that?"

"Why is it that Trace received a warning, but I got a ticket?"

"You would've preferred I wrote up your friend?"

"Nice try."

Grace sighed. "What do you want me to say? I won't apologize for doing my job."

"See, that's the thing...I would've expected you to be more consistent." He saw the moment she realized he'd pushed her into a corner. She blinked and glanced away. "And frankly, more fair."

Her gaze shot back to him. "I don't give locals a pass and zing out-of-towners, if that's what you're implying."

"You know what I mean. I'm referring to the McAllisters. You've been here, what...two weeks...and already you're bowing to them."

"What?" She gaped at him. Her astonishment wasn't an act. "What are you talking about?"

"I want to know why you let Trace off and not me," he said, no longer sure he'd pegged her correctly.

She gave him a long, hard look. "Are you trying to get me to void the ticket? Is that what this is about?"

"No." Leaning in, hoping to lighten things up, he asked, "Is it working?"

She smiled a little. "Look, Ben, let's not waste each other's time. I know your type."

The words were like a slap in the face. He hadn't been wrong, after all. He sat back, disappointed as hell. He'd been typecast most of his life. Nowadays, he didn't run into that sort of ignorance much, and when he did, he took it in stride. But coming from Grace...

"Is that right?" he asked. "And what type is that?"

"Do I need to spell it out?" She stared him square in the eye. "Fine. The quintessential charmer. The consummate flirt. You think you can sweet-talk your way out of anything. And you're probably quite successful at it. Not this time."

Ben hardly knew what to say. He'd been wrong again. The only thing left was to hit the ball back into her court. "Guess we're even, because I know your type, too."

She held his gaze, waiting out the silence, then finally asked, "Which is?"

"You'd rather do a pole dance than tear up a ticket."

Grace let out a loud laugh, then briefly covered her mouth. "You really underestimate me." She cleared her throat. "How did you come up with that one? A pole dance?"

He smiled. "A man can dream, can't he?"

"Pole dance," she muttered, shaking her head. Someone drew her attention toward the bar, and she nodded.

"Your friend show up?"

"Who?" She frowned at Ben. "Oh, Clarence. No." After taking another sip, she lowered her gaze along with the beer. "I think I let Trace skate because I was so relieved it wasn't you."

He thought for a moment, not sure what she meant. "Huh."

She looked up. "Don't make me regret admitting it."

Ben smiled at the light blush spreading across her cheeks. "I'll work on that."

"Please do," she said in a dry tone. "How long are you in town for?"

"Maybe a week, give or take."

"You going back to LA?"

He nodded, still confused over her comment about being relieved it was Trace driving. Though he doubted he'd get an explanation. "LA's been home for fifteen years."

"You don't miss Montana?"

"Hollywood has its upside. Though I don't live there anymore. I moved to Valencia."

"I've never been to California. When I was a kid, I begged to go to Disneyland." Her smile dimmed. "It didn't work out."

"So go now."

"I'm a little past that stage. Blackfoot Falls is more my speed."

He didn't believe that. And neither did she, judging by the wistful look in her eyes. "Wait till you've been living here a few months. Disneyland will start looking good." He saw it again, that small seed of doubt before she shuttered her expression. "Where are you from?"

"Arizona. A town not far from Tucson."

"Why the move here? Not for your uncle."

"No," she agreed. "I didn't know him very well before coming here. But he said there was an opening in the sheriff's department, and here I am." She lifted her mug, pausing midway to her lips. "I'm very grateful to him for recommending me. I hope I didn't give you a wrong impression."

"You took care of that by writing me a ticket."

"Oh, and you bore no responsibility by driving like a lunatic."

Ben grinned. "Were you in law enforcement in Arizona?"

She nodded and took a long time to sip a small amount of beer. The waitress stopped at the table, and there was no missing the faint sheen of relief in Grace's eyes. "What do I owe you?"

He did a double take at the petite brunette. Trace's fiancée? "Nikki?"

"Hey, Ben. I saw you at the Sundance this morning, but you left before I could catch you." She winced at the sound of her name being yelled from the back room. "Anyway, Trace and I were hoping we could get together before you left. For drinks, dinner, whatever. You, too, Grace...we can make it a foursome—" Another shout had Nikki sighing.

Ben glanced at Grace for her reaction. Whatever she thought of the idea, she kept it to herself.

"Would you excuse me while I go teach that cowboy some manners?" Nikki said with a deceptively sweet smile.

"Go get 'em."

Grace hurriedly put money on Nikki's tray. "That should cover me, right?"

Nikki gave it back to her. "Your beer's on the house."

More hollering cut off Grace's objection. Her eyes shooting daggers, Nikki stormed for the pool tables. With a hand on her hip, she got in some guy's face.

Ben had met her last night. "She's perfect for Trace," he said, looking at Grace.

She seemed annoyed about the free drink. He noticed she'd slyly tucked a bill under her half-empty mug. He hoped she wasn't leaving.

"I really like her," Grace said, glancing and smiling at the cowboy who sheepishly scratched his head as Nikki gave him an earful. "Between her and Sadie, I understand the place rarely gets too rowdy." She turned back to him and frowned. "Why the smirk?"

"Poor bastards. Now that you're added to the mix, they don't stand a chance."

The corners of her lips twitched. "No, they don't." She shook her head, and some wisps escaped her slicked-back hair. She tried to tame a stubborn curl that kept getting in her eye, and damned if that innocent move didn't light a fire in his groin. "Have you eaten yet?"

"Me?"

Ben smiled at her widened eyes. "How about the diner? The food used to be good."

"It still is. I've eaten there a lot. Aren't you staying at the Sundance?"

"No. They had their hands full with Rachel's friends. I figured it was easier to stay here in town."

She blinked at him, a tiny frown forming between her brows. "So you must be at The Boarding House."

"Is that a problem?"

"No. Not at all. Some of Matt's rodeo buddies are staying there, too. And a distant cousin of Mrs. McAllister. You probably know her from before. I can't remember her name. Anyway, she and her husband left today."

It took him a moment to figure out why the sudden nervous chatter. "Did you find a place yet?"

"Nope." She averted her eyes.

"Staying with your uncle?"

"God, no."

That left only one other place. "The Boarding House?"

"Yep." She lifted the mug to her lips. "It's home for now," she said and took a sip.

"Which room?"

Almost choking on the beer, she lowered the mug. With the tip of her tongue, she swept the foam from the corner of her mouth. Mesmerizing him once again, only this time his cock jumped. "Why?"

"Just curious."

She eyed him warily. "The owner remodeled a suite for herself, but since she's living elsewhere, she's renting it to me."

"That doesn't tell me which room."

"No, it doesn't."

"Afraid I'm going to break in? I know a better way to get into a woman's room." Ben smiled at her deadpan expression and steady gaze. "I'd be happy to demonstrate."

"You're trying to annoy me. It won't work."

"Why would I do that?"

"Um, let's see…because I gave you a ticket?"

"Already forgotten. Come on, let's go eat. I'm starving." He wasn't surprised when she shook her head. "Forget the diner. Kalispell must have some decent restaurants. How about it, Deputy? I promise not to speed."

She smiled a little. "Nope. I work tomorrow."

"I'll get you home early."

"It's already late. Go bother Katy."

"Who?" But then he remembered and automatically looked over at the brunette. She waved. Hell, he wasn't going to mess with Rachel's friends. Mostly because he wasn't interested. He turned his attention back to Grace. "Give that hard-ass image a break. Having a meal with me won't kill you."

She let out a little sigh of exasperation. In response, he bumped his knee against hers under the table.

Her eyes narrowed into a glare. "Stop it," she said, her gaze panning the room. "I mean it. You want to flirt and be cute, I'm sure you'll have women lining up."

He moved his leg. She was serious, and contrary to what she thought, he didn't want to piss her off.

"Ben Carter," someone bellowed. "You sly dog."

Ben recognized the voice. He looked around and saw Buster Hadley standing under the archway to the back room. His former hell-raising buddy still wore his sandy-blond hair in the same shaggy style he'd favored in high school. The guy had always been big and brawny, but now he had a gut on him. Ben didn't bother correcting him on the name. It was pointless. Everyone knew him as Carter.

"Someone told me you were in town," Buster said, heading straight to him. "I think it was Lenny. You remember Lenny from the Circle K."

Ben stood and they shook hands. The guy still had a grip like a vise. "How you doing, Buster?"

"Me?" He snorted. "Hell, I'm married, got two kids. Both boys. Worse troublemakers than you and me were, and they ain't even in high school yet." He barely stopped for a breath. "You still living out there in Hollywood?" He leaned back to size Ben up and let out a low whistle. "Well, look at you, son. You must be getting laid every night."

Ben laughed. "I see you haven't changed. Your wife ever get a word in?"

"Nah, she don't wanna talk to me." His face was flushed, his breath stinking of beer. He clapped Ben on the shoulder. "So, what are you up to? Let me buy you a beer, maybe shoot some pool."

Ben nodded at Grace, who was watching them with curious fascination. "Buster, have you met Grace, the new deputy?"

Buster squinted at her. "Oh yeah…I know who you are. You're taking the sheriff's place, aren't you?"

"I don't know about that," she said with a strained smile.

Right. Noah was leaving. Grace moving here finally made sense to Ben. "It's an elected position, isn't it?" He directed the question to Grace, but Buster answered.

"Yeah, we gotta vote on it this fall. Good old Wade's already started sucking up to everybody. He quit on Noah a few months back because he thought Noah was never gonna leave. You remember Wade…" he said to Ben. "The crybaby was a year behind us in school. Always complaining that the coach kept him on the bench."

Grace fidgeted, likely uncomfortable with the conversation. She was too professional to be gossiping about a coworker. Another reason Ben didn't see her fitting in here. He'd bet she was overqualified for the job. So was Noah, but he grew up in Blackfoot Falls and understood the culture.

A Keith Urban song suddenly roared from the jukebox's speakers. Buster said something that Ben didn't hear because he was too preoccupied with Grace. She'd pushed back from the table and gotten to her feet.

"Hey, man, sorry I interrupted," Buster said. "I didn't mean to start flapping my jaws."

"No problem," Grace said, smiling. "I was getting ready to leave, anyway."

Ben waited for her to meet his eyes. "What about dinner?"

"I already ate." Her gaze skittered away. She was lying. "Nice meeting you, Buster."

"Likewise." He sucked in his gut and moved aside to give her room while slyly eyeing her backside. "Hell, you'll get my vote for sheriff." He grinned. "A pretty thing like you, I expect you'll get all the votes you need."

Grace's smiled wavered briefly. Most people wouldn't have noticed, but Ben had been watching her too closely to miss it.

"Oh, I don't know, I'm not sure if hanging out with Ben helps or hurts my cred around here." She kept her tone light, but he had the feeling she might really be concerned. "Something tells me I should stay as far away from him as possible. What do you think, Buster?" she asked, her eyes staying on Ben, her lips lifted in a slight challenge.

Oblivious to the undercurrent between them, Buster chuckled. "You might be right about that. Ben always had a knack for finding trouble."

Ben smiled. "Would that be you, Grace? Are you going to bring me trouble?"

She blinked, and the fight seemed to leave her. He'd turned the tables on her and expected a witty comeback. She just sighed. "I hope not," she said. "I truly hope not."

GRACE DIDN'T KNOW why she'd bothered rushing to the Food Mart before it closed. Her appetite was gone. And even if she got hungry later, she still had cheese and apples in the small dorm-size refrigerator in her room.

The Boarding House halls were narrow, just as they'd been in the early 1900s. Beth, the owner, had put a lot of thought into the renovations, keeping much of the architecture and decor original, and Grace appreciated the old-time feel to the place. Halfway to her room, she shifted the groceries to her other arm and dug in her pocket for her key. The bag was heavy. She'd bought way too much. Normally, she wasn't a mindless shopper. But she'd been too busy thinking about Ben and how he confused her.

"Let me give you a hand with that."

"Jesus." She jumped at the unexpected sound of his voice, and would've dropped everything if Ben hadn't caught the bag. "You scared the hell out of me."

"Sorry. I thought you saw me." The back of his knuckles grazed her breast as they wrestled over the brown paper sack. "I'll hang on to this while you find your key."

"Hang on to... Oh." She suddenly felt disoriented, all her focus centered on her tightened nipples. Had she come down the wrong hall? She glanced at the number on the door. No, this was her room. "What are you doing here?"

"That's my room right there." He nodded at the next door. "Don't give me that look," he said with a lazy smile. "I didn't ask for a particular room."

"You could've switched," she muttered and stuck her key in the lock.

Ben's low, rumbling laugh sounded too sexy for her peace of mind. "You must think you're pretty damn irresistible."

Heat surged to her cheeks. "Thank you. I'll take the bag."

"You are, you know. Irresistible." He refused to let go, and she refused to look at him. He was too close. She could feel his warm breath on her face. "Grace?"

She gripped the bag only to hear the paper tear. Voices and laughter carried from the tiny lobby. The inn was small. Any moment, someone could come down the hall.

"Invite me in," Ben whispered.

The voices grew louder.

Grace turned the key and pushed open the door. She spun around to take the bag from him. He'd already slipped in behind her, so she stepped back, and he shut the door.

"I figured you wouldn't want people thinking I'd just

left your room," he said as she flipped on the light switch in time to see that oh-so-charming smile of his.

"How considerate of you."

He moved closer, smelling faintly of mint and warm male flesh. "Shall I put this by the fridge?"

"I'll take it."

Again, his fingers lightly brushed her breast, and she jerked a look at his expressionless face. It obviously was an accident, but that didn't stop the tingling from going all the way down to her thighs.

She set the groceries on the small oak table and noticed the four-inch gap between the green brocade drapes. Great. Anyone driving down Main Street curious enough to look could see them. She pulled the two sides of the fabric together until they overlapped.

"Much better," Ben said, his tone laced with amusement. "It's nice and cozy in here."

"Too bad you won't be staying."

"I will if you ask nicely."

Grace ignored him and listened for voices in the hall. A door closed. Otherwise, it was quiet. "Where's Buster?"

"At The Watering Hole." Ben eyed the small love seat and side table that wasn't much wider than the base of the lamp it held. The kitchen consisted of a short counter, sink, minifridge and microwave. "I might have to give him a ride home." He looked at the closed door to the adjoining room. "The bedroom?"

She nodded, hating the edgy feeling she couldn't shake. Somehow Ben seemed bigger, taller, his shoulders broader in this small room with its pint-size furniture.

She folded her arms across her chest. "The rooms are all the same except this one is set up like a parlor."

"It's not bad for a short stay." He glanced over at her, his gaze lingering for a moment on her tightly crossed arms. "Are you looking for a house?"

"I haven't really thought about it. I doubt I'll have much of a choice. There aren't many rentals available."

"What about Noah? Is he renting a place you could take over?"

"The sheriff's compensation package includes a house. If whoever is elected doesn't want it, I bet the county will rent it out." She could barely think about Wade getting the position. "So maybe I'll end up renting it..." She trailed off, sighed.

"I can't see you sticking around as a deputy."

"You don't even know me."

His gaze briefly drifted down the front of her blouse before returning to her face. "I know enough."

She wasn't sure how to interpret that, but it made her step back. "If Buster's too drunk to drive, should you really leave him to his own devices?"

"Sadie has his keys." Ben smiled. "Are you trying to get rid of me, Grace?"

"I never invited you in to begin with," she said, irritated when all he did was laugh. "Look, if you need a plaything while you're in town doing whatever it is you're here to do, then I suggest you find someone who—" She stopped, confused by the sudden disappointment in his face.

"And here I thought you were above gossip."

She'd hit a nerve. Unintentional, but nevertheless. "You're right. I don't gossip. I was speaking in general terms."

"General terms?"

She shrugged. "Someone who leaves home and stays away for fifteen years usually has a reason."

The amusement was back in his eyes. "You mean like someone who moves to a Podunk town in the middle of nowhere for a job she can do in her sleep?"

She resisted the impulse to strike back. "Touché."

"That's it?"

Grace smiled. "That's it."

"Then you'd better do something about that leak."

"The what?" She turned to the sack of groceries. Vanilla ice cream seeped from the corner of the brown paper. "Oh, great."

She grabbed the bag and moved it to the sink. A stream of ice cream ran down the inside of her forearm. Ben was right behind her with the roll of paper towels. He mopped the drips off the floor while she salvaged what she could from the bag.

Stepping aside so he could use the sink, she licked the stickiness from her fingers. "Thank you," she said, trying to keep out of his way. "I can finish."

"Wait." He caught her arm, trapping her between him and the counter.

She held her breath as he leaned close, his face inches from her own. "Ben." She gripped the counter behind her, watching his eyes darken. "What are you doing?"

He touched the side of her mouth with his thumb, showed her the trace of ice cream he'd swept away, then brushed it across her lower lip. Her tongue slipped out to blot the sweetness. He watched the movement with an expression of utter fascination.

Grace hadn't consciously moved closer, but her left thigh pressed against his right one and her palm rested on his chest. She tried to swallow, but her mouth was too dry.

"Relax, Grace. I won't hurt you."

As if he could, she thought with a scratchy laugh that only exacerbated her desperate need to swallow. "Ben," she whispered.

"Yes?" he murmured against the side of her neck, his warm lips setting off sparks of excitement.

She felt his hand at the back of her head releasing her hair from the clip. "You have to leave."

"You sure about that?"

She closed her eyes as he nipped at her lobe. Want and panic battled inside her. To let him continue was asking for trouble. No way could she rationalize this behavior. Not with her future at stake.

With a gentle finger, he lifted her chin, tipped her face up and placed his mouth over hers. He teased her lips, slow and deliberate, tasting and testing, then firming as she responded. One hand moved down her back. The other skimmed the curve of her hip. Want surged under his touch, and she pressed into his aroused body, opening her mouth to his insistent tongue.

He yanked her blouse from her jeans, and she went for his belt. She couldn't make her clumsy hands work. The fumbling and frustration cooled her off some, allowing reason to break through the fog. What the hell was she doing? Too much was at stake for her to veer off the path even for a minute. Ben had a murky reputation, and he'd be gone soon anyway.

She stepped back, caught her breath. "Ben," she said, drawing his name out into an apology. "I can't."

He stared at her for a moment, then closed his eyes briefly. "Pity," he said, retucking his shirt. "You were doing just fine."

6

THE NEXT MORNING, Ben tried to reach his partner for the third time. Not only was Lena not picking up, she hadn't returned his calls. She was in between boy toys and probably still angry with him for leaving and not accompanying her to the fund-raiser she'd cohosted. That wouldn't surprise him. They were friends, in loose Hollywood terms, and he never minded standing in as her escort, so she often counted on him. But pulling this petty crap in the middle of a business deal? That wasn't like Lena.

He left another message, then drove out to the Sundance. On the way, he thought about calling Grace and asking her out tonight. But he figured she wouldn't take his call while on duty, and leaving a voice mail would be stupid. Too easy for her to ignore him.

Deputy Grace Hendrix was going to need some coaxing. If he caught her off guard, he might have a shot at opening up negotiations. He smiled, thinking that was exactly what it would take with her.

Grace was something new. Not just a challenge, but a bit of a mystery. She wasn't just some small-town gal from the Arizona desert like she'd have him believe. The woman had steel in her spine. Her reaction to Buster last night had been something to watch. She'd processed and evaluated his sexist remark in the blink of an eye and let it go.

A woman with her iron self-control might have something interesting to hide. He had to give her props, though, for doing it well. He imagined she did a lot of things well.

She'd shut him down last night, but the two of them, they were going to tango.

His certainty didn't come from arrogance. It was their kiss, her soft breathy moans as she'd slid her arms around his waist and clung to him. It was the startled look in her eyes that told him she hadn't expected her own response. No way things between them could end there. Not for him. Not for either of them.

Last night had left him feeling restless, edgy, as if he had unfinished business that needed to be settled. The sensation wouldn't go away. Halfway to the Sundance, Ben almost gave in and called her cell. Something made him glance at the speedometer, and he immediately lifted his foot off the accelerator. He wanted to see her, but not while she wrote him another ticket.

Trace was already working with a black gelding when Ben arrived. He parked the Porsche in the shade and headed straight for the corral.

"What are you doing up so early?" Trace asked, grinning. "It's only eleven-thirty."

"The altitude must be messing with my head." Ben propped a foot on the bottom rail and glanced at the animal in the next corral. "You guys keeping mustangs now?"

"Nah. I've been helping with the roundups, and that one caught my eye. I need to work with him, but I'm trying to get this stubborn son-of-a-bitch saddle broke first."

"You still move cattle on horseback?"

"I do, and so do Jesse and Dutch. But nowadays most of the men prefer four-wheelers. Josh...he came after you left...sometimes he uses a dirt bike to ride the fences."

It made some sense. Gas was probably cheaper in the

long run. But for him, there was no substitute for a fine horse. "You been on him yet?"

"Twice." Trace eyed the gelding. "I've eaten some dirt thanks to you, huh, Maverick?"

The black shifted to the right and eyed him with mistrust.

Ben laughed. "Yep, got him eating out of the palm of your hand."

"I will," Trace said, his attention focused on the gelding. "Sooner or later. Just takes some patience. Right, boy?"

"Want me to give it a try?"

"I heard about you buying a ranch," Trace said. "But when was the last time you rode a horse that wasn't saddle-broke?"

"I've been a stunt man for twelve years. When you go see a Western, who do you think is hitting the dirt in a rodeo scene? Those A-list actors aren't looking to get their pretty faces messed up."

"What about that mug of yours? How many times you get your nose broken?"

"Only once. My jaw twice." Ben probed the spot. It had happened a while back, but sometimes the joint still ached. So yeah, maybe he'd leave Maverick to Trace.

The sound of an engine made them both turn their heads. A small silver compact drove down the driveway.

"I don't recognize the car," Trace said, watching until the vehicle got closer. "Oh, it's the new deputy. The one who stopped me yesterday."

Ben knew it was Grace because he'd seen her sneak away from the wedding in that car. But why wasn't she working?

"Probably here to see Nikki." Trace returned his attention to Maverick. "I understand you might be buying stock from us. Are we talking horses, cattle?"

"Why isn't she driving the truck?" Ben murmured,

watching her park in the shade a respectful distance from the Porsche. "She's supposed to be on duty."

After a silence, Trace asked, "How do you know Grace? Other than her writing you up."

"I talked to her at the party." Ben shrugged. "And at The Watering Hole last night."

"She still wouldn't rip up your ticket?"

"I didn't ask her to."

Trace gave him a look of pure amusement. "She's pretty."

"Let me see what I can do with Maverick," Ben said and slipped between the rails of the corral.

"You sure you wanna do that?" Trace glanced back at Grace, his mouth curving in a smile.

Ben knew what Trace was thinking, but he didn't need to ride a bucking bronc to impress a woman. And he sure as hell wasn't about to let Trace goad him.

"Easy, boy." Ben patiently stroked the gelding's side and flank, murmuring softly until he felt it was time to mount.

He swung into the saddle. The black reared and pawed the air like he was being dragged into hell. Ben tightened his hold on the reins, but it was too late. The gelding bucked a few times, sending Ben over his head. Luckily, he landed on his ass.

Grinning, Trace offered him a hand up.

Ben ignored it and sprang to his feet.

"You wanna try that again?" Trace asked, hooting with laughter. "This is child's play for you, Mr. Studman...oh, I mean stunt man."

"Shut the hell up." Ben dusted himself off while covertly trying to locate Grace. She'd stopped at the edge of the corral, shading her eyes and watching him.

"Come on, dude, you know what they say about getting right back in the saddle," Trace said, barely managing to get the words out through his laughter.

"Jesus, Trace. Grow up."

"No fun in that."

Ben shook his head. "Fifteen years and you're still the same pain in the ass."

"Mighty comforting to know some things never change, isn't it?" Trace wiped his eyes with the back of his wrist. "I needed a good belly laugh. Oh, and I should've warned you. Maverick doesn't like it when you whisper too close to his ear."

"Yeah, thanks." Ben stomped his foot to get some of the dirt off his boot, his very expensive boot. He sent more dust flying. "I should make you pay for these."

Trace snorted. "The dirt's an improvement," he said, eyeing Ben's Lucchese python boots. "You look like a god-damned greenhorn in that fancy footwear."

"I give up." Sighing, Ben turned to Grace, who stood off to the side. Her hair brushed her shoulders, a little wild, as if she'd been plowing her hands through the shiny loose curls. "I thought you were working."

"Uh, no, I— Are you okay?"

"Fine."

She studied him with a worried frown, then smiled at Trace. "Hi."

"Mornin'," Trace said, leading Maverick to the center of the corral. "Is this a social call, or you here to arrest him?" Grinning, he nodded at Ben.

Grace gave Ben a sizing-up. "Did he do something I should know about?"

"Well, now." Trace adjusted his Stetson. "I'd say that's likely a given."

"Come on, Grace, make my day," Ben said. "Tell me you changed your mind and you're here to give the kid a ticket."

"Hey, hold on there," Trace grumbled. "I'm not a kid."

Grace laughed. But as soon as she turned to Ben, her gaze flickered, her smile fading. She dragged her palms down the front of her snug-fitting jeans. "I'm supposed to meet Nikki and Rachel here."

"Rachel?" Ben brushed the dust off his chambray shirt. "No honeymoon?"

"Matt can't afford to leave now," Trace said. "You know how busy it is in the spring." He nodded at Grace. "Everybody's inside. Go through the front door or to the kitchen. You don't have to knock."

"Thanks." She briefly glanced at Ben and then started for the house.

"Wait," he said and jumped the corral railing.

She hesitated, just long enough to irritate him, then slowly turned around.

Aware that Trace was watching them, Ben caught up to her and spoke in a low voice. "You lied about working today."

"I didn't lie. I was just confused about my schedule."

"Right." As if he'd buy that.

"Whatever." With a dismissive shrug, she turned to go.

"Hold on." Another time, another woman, Ben would've walked away. But after last night's kiss, he knew this indifference was just an act. She was new in town. She had to watch her step. He got it. Up to a point. He cocked his chin at the house. "How long are you going to be?"

"They want my input for a going-away party for Noah. I don't know why. I barely know him."

"A surprise party?" Ben asked, and she nodded. "Noah isn't going to like that."

"Really?" Grace winced. "Rachel should know that, right? I don't want to make him angry."

"He knows how Rachel is. Noah won't blame you." Ben sensed that Grace was really worried. "You won't be working with him much longer."

"No, but he'll have a say in who—" She turned away again. "I should go. They must be waiting."

He caught her wrist. "Tell them you can't stay long,"

he said, enjoying the feel of her soft skin. "That we have plans."

"But we don't."

"Easy to rectify." Her pulse quickened under his thumb. "How about we pick up where we left off last night?"

She pulled her arm away. "That can't happen again."

"What? Kissing?"

She took a step back. And then another. "I'm sure you understand."

A door slammed. They both turned their heads. It was only Chester, the bunkhouse cook, carrying a Dutch oven from the house.

But Grace took off before Ben could say another word.

RACHEL AND HER MOTHER, Barbara, sat at the kitchen table making lists while Nikki and Hilda fixed rolled tacos that smelled like heaven. Most of the details for Noah's party had already been worked out, which made Grace wonder why Rachel had invited her. She thought about Ben and hoped this wasn't a matchmaking effort.

She sighed at her own foolishness. Her and Ben? No one in their right mind would consider the possibility.

"What about parking?" Nikki asked.

Rachel looked up. "What about it?"

"He'll see the cars and know it's not just dinner with the family."

Rachel groaned.

Barbara sighed and massaged her temples. "I'm not sure I've recovered from Saturday night yet."

Hilda stood at the sink, sneaking peeks out the window. Just as she'd done many times in the twenty minutes since Grace arrived.

"For what it's worth," she said, "Ben thinks Noah will hate being surprised."

"Oh yeah, I know." Rachel shrugged. "He'll get over it."

"Is he coming inside?" Hilda asked, turning anxiously to Grace. "My son. Did he say anything to you?"

"Um, not really."

The woman's eyes dimmed, and Grace's heart twisted. After not seeing Ben for so long, it was probably difficult for Hilda to share him with everyone.

"I know what we can do," Rachel said. "Instead of using the family dinner ruse, we can tell Noah it's a party for Ben. That'll explain all the cars."

"That won't work." Barbara shook her head. "Not unless we can be ready in two days. Ben's leaving."

Hilda's shoulders slumped. Grace's own disappointment caught her off guard. Two days? Hadn't he said a week? It shouldn't matter, and yet she'd stopped listening to the conversation. Her brain wasn't the only part of her body having a reaction. Memories of last night's kiss were never far from her thoughts, causing all sorts of flutters in her tummy.

"What I don't like about being married to Matt," Rachel announced snagging everyone's attention, "is that I miss Hilda's cooking. I swear, you are the best cook in the whole world." Rachel left her chair and gave Hilda a hug.

"And to think, once upon a time, Hilda couldn't even boil water," Barbara said with a laugh. "Literally. She kept playing with the stove knobs."

Hilda was smiling now. "I was so helpless, I had to learn how to fry eggs, of all things."

"Why have I not heard this before?" Rachel seemed surprised, though more interested in the tacos. "Would you like me to sample one of these? Just to make sure the seasoning is right."

Making a clucking sound, Hilda slapped her hand away.

Rachel uttered a token protest and cast a sly glance out the window. "Aren't these tacos Ben's favorite? Someone should go get him." She looked at Grace. "Would you mind?"

Startled, and not altogether happy, Grace shrugged. So this was a matchmaking attempt, after all. Much as she wanted to, she couldn't very well refuse. "All right," she said, getting to her feet.

Hilda's face lit up and it hit Grace that this little ploy had nothing to do with her. It was for Ben's mom's benefit. Had they argued? Was she upset over his short stay?

"Wait, please, Grace. Not yet." Hilda rushed to the stainless steel refrigerator. "I still have to make the guacamole and salsa."

"We already have a large container of salsa," Barbara said as she rose. "I'll chop the onions and mash the avocados."

Shaking her head, Hilda grabbed ingredients from the fridge. "Ben likes the one with the green chilies."

Barbara and Rachel exchanged sympathetic looks.

"We'll all help," Nikki said calmly, making room on the counter. "While we figure out what to do about Noah's party."

Barbara handed Grace a bag of fresh tomatoes, a knife and cutting board. She went to work chopping, thinking about how she wasn't used to being around women all that much. While she wasn't terribly useful in a kitchen, she managed okay with what she'd learned from her father. Though they'd eaten a lot of burgers, hot dogs and beans after her mom died.

Her phone buzzed, and she stopped to read the text. Ben. The flutter kicked in again. She glanced guiltily around the kitchen, which was stupid. Neither texting nor Ben was illegal, though maybe he should be.

Dinner? was all the message said.

Grace couldn't help but smile as she slipped the phone back into her pocket. Persistent devil. She couldn't deny she was flattered. Except he didn't mean just dinner.

So she really had to think about this. Knowing he'd be gone in two days did put a different spin on things. If they were careful, no one would know. And she'd done without for too long. Plus, after he left, she'd likely be in for another dry spell.

Sure, there were a number of cowboys working at the surrounding ranches. Though no one who interested her enough to deal with the hassle of dating in front of the whole town. Living in Blackfoot Falls could feel like living in a fishbowl for a single woman deputy. Especially for one who aspired to be sheriff.

Wow, that was depressing.

She hadn't thought about that aspect of the move before.

Grace made up her mind. She was going for it. So what that she wasn't a starlet or a model, the kind of woman Ben undoubtedly went for. He wasn't her type, either. But the way he'd kissed her left her weak in the knees.

She finished chopping tomatoes, only half listening to the lively discussion around her. By the time she cleaned up her mess and washed her hands, Hilda had made the guacamole and added the tomatoes to the salsa.

"Grace, will you let the other deputies know the day and time of the party?" Rachel asked. "I'm not putting anything on paper. I don't trust those bozos not to leave it around for Noah to see." She briefly covered her mouth. "Oops. Sorry."

"What?" Grace smiled. "Did you say something?"

Rachel laughed. "I think we're ready for Ben. You mind?"

"Not at all." Grace looked at Hilda. Her anxious expression made Grace swallow. Ben had so little time here. He should be having dinner with his mom, not her.

She headed out the back door and spotted Trace right away. He stood outside the corral, deep in conversation with an older man, their gazes trained on the gelding.

Ben was nowhere in sight.

She strained to see if the Porsche was still there. Yep. Her breath caught. She saw him. Helping Katy into the passenger seat.

7

GRACE WAITED UNTIL 3:30 p.m. to go to the office, when the shifts overlapped and she could tell everyone about Noah's party at the same time. Roy and Danny were just about to go off duty. Technically, Wade was already on the clock when she walked in, but he was lounging in Noah's chair, drinking coffee. He leaned back with a cocky smirk and propped his boots on the edge of Noah's desk.

God, could he be more obvious in staking his claim? Roy and Danny weren't nearly as bad. She honestly didn't know how they could stand him. But then, he'd been smart enough to claim the role of pack leader.

"What are you doing here on your day off? Sucking up?" Wade asked. "You picked the wrong day. Noah is in Missoula until tomorrow morning."

"I know. But if I hadn't, I would've guessed." Grace smiled pointedly at Wade's boots, then turned to Roy and Danny. "The McAllisters are having a get-together for Noah a week from Thursday. It's a surprise, so don't say anything."

Roy chuckled. "Those folks sure like their parties. Do we bring our wives?"

Grace nodded. "Weather permitting, it'll be a barbecue."

"How do you know about it?"

Hearing the anger in Wade's voice, she wished she'd let Roy pass on the information. But with Noah gone, this had been the perfect opportunity to make sure they all knew. "Rachel told me," Grace said. "Can one of you tell Gus?"

"I suppose you just ran into her?" Wade said, a scowl on his thin face.

Now Danny was frowning at her, as well, his initial curiosity turning into an accusation.

"No, I saw her at the Sundance." Why they cared that she knew about the party first was beyond her comprehension. Heaven forbid they found out Rachel had included her in the planning. Theoretically, because she hadn't added much.

"What were you doing out there?" Wade got to his feet. "You sucking up to the McAllisters, too?"

"Yeah, that's right, Wade." Grace sighed. What a hell of a day off. First she'd been roped into doing something that would annoy her boss. Then Ben had ditched her, and now her coworkers were being jerks.

To be fair, Roy didn't seem upset. Or at least he hadn't until now. He'd been writing in the daily log. But there was some sort of silent communication happening between him, Wade and Danny.

She had no desire to stick around and find out what they were conspiring. "Okay, I've passed on the invite. Try to keep it secret for Rachel's sake."

"Yes, ma'am. Whatever you say." Wade snorted. "Practicing how it feels to be sheriff?"

She paused at the door, telling herself it was best to ignore him. Then she turned back with a smile. "I wasn't the one trying out his chair and desk."

Roy barked out a laugh. Danny might have gotten in a chuckle, too. She wasn't sure, because she left the office without glancing back. Something she should've done in the first place. She'd seen Wade's face flush a dark red, and now she wanted to kick herself. She knew better than to participate in petty stuff like that.

Besides, she still had to work with the guy. And it was possible he'd be named the interim sheriff. If that happened, she'd quit. Find someplace else to lick her wounds.

It was Ben's fault that she wasn't herself. He had some nerve asking her to dinner one minute, then taking off with Katy the next. He hadn't even waited for Grace's answer. Of course, she hadn't texted him back after seeing him leave with the brunette. So her dignity remained somewhat intact. But damn it, she'd looked forward to seeing him tonight. Instead, she would end up reading another mystery.

She'd walked the few blocks from The Boarding House to the office, which had been pleasant. The return trip, not so much. She scowled past the bank, the bar and the *Salina Gazette* office before forcing herself to smile at the next passerby. A minute later, a black truck slowed beside her, the ubiquitous vehicle and color a Blackfoot Falls favorite. She didn't know who it was until the tinted glass lowered.

"Hey, Hendrix." Roy hung an arm out the window. "You doing anything later?"

"Why?" She stayed where she was on the opposite sidewalk. "You know it's a crime to lynch a fellow deputy."

Roy grinned. "Danny and I are going to The Watering Hole at around six-thirty. Meet us there."

"What for?"

"A few beers, some pool, whatever. We go twice a month."

She hesitated, though she didn't see the harm. Roy hadn't been a jerk. Wade was on the job, so he wouldn't be there. She did wonder about Danny but trusted Roy would've cleared it with him before asking her.

"Okay," she said finally. "Six-thirty."

"Good. I gotta have supper with the wife and kids, but I'll be there by six forty-five at the latest."

Grace watched him drive down Main, stopping twice

to talk to people on the street before he turned off for the highway. They better not be setting her up for a repeat of last night. Sitting alone and waiting like an idiot wouldn't be the worst thing to happen…unless Ben showed up with Katy draped over him.

THE JUKEBOX BLARED extra loud, though the bar wasn't horribly crowded. Grace liked country music as well as the next person, but she was beginning to wonder if the big antique Wurlitzer had any other selections.

"Hey, Sam!" With his head turned toward the pool players, Roy leaned back and cupped his hands around his mouth. "Sam Miller, get your tail over here and meet the new deputy."

"Oh, no. Please don't." Grace stared at her hands and grabbed her mug. "We've already met."

Roy and Danny exchanged knowing looks and burst out laughing.

"Sam hit on you already?" Roy asked. "I lost count of how many shotguns he's had pulled on him by pissed-off daddies."

"Really?" Was he joking? It was hard to tell. "They do that here?"

"Nah, not too often," Danny said. "I mean, Sam's had a couple, maybe three run-ins, but that's it. I had to tell him to stay away from my kid sister." He shrugged his beefy shoulders and swept back a lock of brown hair that fell across his forehead. "She got mad when she found out. But Lynn's only nineteen."

Grace smiled at him. Danny was big and husky, still young himself, maybe twenty-four at the most. And she'd discovered he could be very sweet. "It's nice that you look out for your sister. I always wished I had a brother."

"You got only sisters?"

"Nope. Just me." She saw that Roy was still trying to

get Sam's attention. "If he comes over, I'm leaving," she warned.

"Ah, he didn't hear me," Roy said. "He's busy shooting pool."

She sipped her beer and grimaced. It tasted funny. She probably should ask the waitress, Gretchen, for another. But Roy and Danny were drinking the same thing, and they said their beers were fine. Though they'd each downed a shot, too, so maybe their taste buds weren't so reliable.

Danny motioned for Gretchen to bring another round.

"Not for me," Grace said. "Two's enough."

"Come on…" Danny grinned. "At least do a shot with us."

She laughed. "Nope. I work tomorrow morning."

"Just one." Danny slid Roy a mischievous look.

"No." She shook her head. "Won't happen, so forget it."

A Blake Shelton song ended, followed by another that blasted from the Wurlitzer.

"Where are you going?" Danny asked when she stood.

She suddenly needed to take a moment. It wasn't that she was dizzy exactly. Or drunk. A tad fuzzy maybe, though she'd eaten dinner before she'd come to the bar. "Does the jukebox take quarters?"

"Yep," Roy said and reached into his pocket.

"I've got it." Grace gave the table a wide berth. She felt giddy. She never felt giddy. So maybe that was the wrong word. Anyway, she was pleased to be included and was actually having fun.

As a bonus, she'd managed to forget about Ben. Almost. He'd popped into her mind a few times, like now. But she wasn't pining for him. Figured she'd finally decided to go for it the same time he'd grown impatient and moved on.

A tall, dark-haired cowboy she'd never seen before walked out of the back room and gave her a smile and a once-over. She peeked at his butt as he passed. Not as nice as Ben's behind, but the guy still looked good.

He stopped and turned. "Do you play pool?"

"No," she said, hoping he hadn't caught her checking him out. "Never tried."

"I can teach you."

Grace laughed. "Okay." She remembered Roy and Danny. "But I can't tonight."

"No problem. I'm Jay."

"Grace."

"I know." He had quite a nice smile and a firm handshake. "Why don't you give me your number and we can set something up?"

It slowly registered that he already knew her name. So of course he knew she was a deputy. He was also holding on to her hand too long. "I come in a couple times a week," she said, and drew back. "We'll see each other again."

He cocked his head and studied her a moment. "You giving me the brush-off, Grace?"

"No. I'm here with people." She started to look over at Roy and Danny, but couldn't stand to see if they were watching.

"All right then," Jay said. "Until next time."

Surprised at herself, she hurried to the jukebox. She hadn't actually flirted, but she had shown interest. That wasn't something she normally did, much less in front of her coworkers. While her personal life was her own business, she wasn't about to give Roy and Danny ammunition to get under her skin. The tension had finally started to ease. And she wanted to keep it that way.

BEN LEANED AGAINST the bar, watching Grace while he waited for his drink. Fine, she had plans, but she could've at least texted him back. He'd just come from an unsettling conversation with his mother. This time, she'd sat with him. Touched him a lot. Teared up a couple times. Hadn't avoided his eyes too much, even when he asked about her family, so that was progress. Though she might've been lying about having no siblings or contact with her parents. Oddly, he didn't think so.

Talking about Claudia had been easier. His mom was excited about going to help with her new grandbaby for a month. Most of his visit with her had gone well. Right up until the last five minutes. And then something she'd said jarred him. About when his father had died. Ben had held his tongue, though, not ready to accuse her of contradicting herself when he could be the one confused.

But right now he focused his attention on the two guys sitting with Grace. His first thought was that they must be deputies, but man, they were too out of shape for that. The heavier one looked vaguely familiar.

"Jack Daniel's. Neat." Sadie set the glass in front of him. "I assume you want to run a tab."

Nodding absently, he saw Grace get to her feet. Something was off with the way she moved. He didn't think she was drunk, but she might've lost her footing. She gripped the edge of the table for a moment before walking toward the jukebox.

"So how long are you here for?" Sadie asked as she wiped down the place next to him.

"A couple more days."

"Quick trip."

"I've got business back in California." Last night he'd recognized Sadie right away, but he didn't really know her. She'd owned the bar for as long as he could remember, and any underage kid with half a brain knew to stay clear. If Sadie caught you sneaking a drink, you prayed she'd call the sheriff. "You still keep a bat behind there?"

"Damn right. And a shotgun."

"Loaded?"

"None of your business."

Ben smiled. "The two guys sitting with Grace, are they deputies?"

Sadie glanced at the table and nodded. "You should

know Roy Tisdale. Probably not Danny. He's too young.
I'm kinda surprised she's socializing with them. Those
boys have been giving her nothing but grief."

"Grace told you?"

"Nah, she's not the type to complain. I heard tales from
Abe over at the variety store, and I believe him. I get the
feeling she's smarter than all of them put together. They
gotta be worried none of them will have a shot at being
elected sheriff."

Sadie moved down to the other end of the bar to refill
mugs. Ben turned back to Grace. He'd looked away for
only a minute, but that's all it had taken for some guy to
hit on her. For a woman concerned about her image, she
didn't seem too put off.

He glanced at her fellow deputies to see how they were
reacting. The waitress had just delivered a round of shots
and beer. The second she left, the younger one—Danny—
dumped a shot into Grace's mug. Roy shook his head, but
he was just as guilty. He'd kept an eye out to make sure
Grace didn't catch them, and now he was laughing along
with his coconspirator.

Stupid bastards. Spiking her beer.

No wonder Grace was so relaxed.

Ben grabbed his drink and joined her at the jukebox.
She nibbled at her lower lip, concentrating hard on the
song selections. His arm brushed hers and she looked up,
startled. When she saw that it was him, her lips lifted in
a dazzling smile, and he felt an odd thump in his chest.

"Hi," she said. "You're here."

"I am." He studied her slightly flushed face. She wasn't
drunk, but she was definitely feeling the effects of the alcohol. He wondered how many shots they'd slipped her.
"Where am I supposed to be?"

She blinked. "You left with Katy."

"Katy?"

"You know, Rachel's friend."

"Yeah, I know who she is." As far as Ben knew, Katy and her two friends had left for the Kalispell airport hours ago.

"This morning," Grace said. "At the Sundance."

"Ah, okay. Her rental car had a flat tire. I went with her to change it."

"Oh. I thought—" Grace shrugged. "It's not important."

Ben noticed a couple hovering behind them. "Are you finished choosing a song? We got people waiting."

"Oh, God." She leaned close enough for him to breathe in the soft scent of her skin. "They'll probably play more country music."

"Which you obviously don't like."

"I like it fine, but you can overdo anything."

"Not entirely true."

Laughing, she wagged a finger at him. "I know what you're implying."

Ben smiled. Oh yeah, she was a little tipsy. "How about we move out of the way," he said, touching her lower back and urging her to the side.

"I'm here with Roy and Danny. They actually invited me. At first, I thought they were mad because Rachel told me about…" Grace glanced around and lowered her voice "…the party for Noah." Leaning closer, she placed a palm on his chest, proof she was feeling the booze. "Maybe they've decided to give me a chance since I've met with the McAllisters' approval."

"You know what I think?"

She gave him that smile again. "What?"

"They're a couple of losers who are just bright enough to be nervous about you running circles around them."

"Don't say that." She glanced over at the two men, their gazes glued to her and Ben. "It was thoughtful of them to include me tonight."

It took all of Ben's willpower not to yank the jerks out of their chairs and punch their lights out. What stopped him was Grace. She looked so happy. She thought they'd finally accepted her. He didn't want to burst her bubble. Later, though, he'd make damn sure they never pulled this stunt again.

"How about I walk you back to The Boarding House?"

"I can't leave. That would be rude. Come join us," she said, her eyes sparkling. "Though I'm not staying much longer. I work tomorrow." Blinking at the hand she'd placed on his chest, she slowly lowered it.

"How much have you had to drink?"

"Two beers." She sounded insulted. "Why?"

Ben shrugged and glanced at the table. Roy and Danny stared at them as if they were watching a damn reality TV show. "I noticed you guys were doing shots."

"Not me." Grace shook her head. "Those two are," she said, looking over her shoulder. "Oh, no, I told them I didn't want another beer."

"You don't have to drink it."

"No. I won't." She turned back to him, worrying her bottom lip, then smiled. "Let's go."

She let him take her arm, though she was perfectly fine to walk. In fact, the only sign she was slightly tipsy was that she was relaxed with him. Just the way he wanted her. But even a bastard like him wouldn't take advantage of her like this.

8

GRACE SHIVERED IN the brisk air and moved closer to Ben. "When do the nights start warming up?"

"I don't remember. I'd guess by June. You cold?"

"Just a little." She rubbed her bare forearms and picked up the pace. "You don't have to walk me back. It's perfectly safe. I am a deputy, after all."

"Soon to be sheriff."

She smiled at him. "I'm an outsider. The odds are against me."

"But you're smarter and more experienced than those other guys."

"You don't know that." It was sweet of him to say, though. "I'm also a woman."

"Huh." His lips twitched. "I hadn't noticed."

Grace laughed and looked up at the dark, overcast sky. Clouds hid half the moon, but she could still see a handful of stars. The stores on this end of Main Street closed by 6:00 p.m. and the only establishment open was the gas station close to The Boarding House. And while the streetlights were few, the lighting was decent.

As they crossed the street and passed the Cut and Curl, she caught her toe on the buckling sidewalk. She righted herself, and didn't mind that Ben cupped her elbow.

"You okay?" he asked.

"Fine." Something in his voice made her give him a long, assessing look, but he wasn't giving away his thoughts. "You don't think I'm drunk, do you? Because I'm not." She paused, waiting for a confirmation or denial. "The sidewalk is uneven. It needs to be repaired."

"Watch out. Here comes another dip," he said, tightening his hold of her arm.

"See?" she said smugly. "I hope you showed Katy how to change her own tire."

Ben looked at Grace and laughed. "Where did that come from?"

"I was thinking about earlier, at the Sundance, when I went to call you for lunch. Your mom had made tacos. I saw Katy get in your Porsche..." Huh. She'd been about to make a point and now it was gone. Poof. She'd lost it.

They reached The Boarding House, and Ben stopped at the porch steps. "Is that why you didn't answer my text?"

"I was going to after I finished chopping tomatoes. Then I saw you with Katy and I figured dinner was out." She started up the steps then turned when she realized he hadn't moved. "Aren't you—?" She cleared her throat. He'd seemed a bit preoccupied on their walk. Probably had other plans. "Okay," she said, trying to hide her disappointment. "I guess this is good-night."

He looked torn. And maybe a little irritable. "I'll walk you to your door."

She waved her hand. "Forget it. I'm fine."

"Don't worry. I won't barge my way into your room."

She didn't like his defensive tone. Was this about last night? She waited until they entered the small lobby and faced him. "What if I invite you in?"

Ben simply stared at her. No smile, his expression blank, his gaze locked on her face. "Come on." He slipped a loose arm around her shoulders and turned her toward the hall.

Annoyed and humiliated by his aloofness, she shook free. "Look, if you don't want to come in, then—"

"Good evening," he said quietly, and he wasn't looking at her.

She followed his gaze to a tiny white-haired lady sitting on a wing chair in the corner, who'd glanced up from her knitting. "Don't mind me," she said. "I'm just waiting on my husband."

Grace managed to smile and didn't object when Ben took her hand. "Just shoot me," she murmured once they were out of earshot.

Ben chuckled. "She didn't hear you."

"I have never seen a person sitting in that lobby. Not once, not in two weeks."

"Even if she heard you, so what? She's a tourist."

"How do you know?"

"You didn't see her whip out a cell phone and call Marge at the diner, did you?"

Grace grinned. "You have a point." She dug her key out of her pocket and immediately dropped it.

He scooped it up and opened her door. "Here." He pressed the cold metal against her palm. "Lock up once you're inside," he said.

"Well, what do you think? I was planning an open house?" Now she was cranky. And very confused.

The condescending curve of his mouth didn't help. "Good night, Grace. Sleep well."

"I should've stayed at The Watering Hole," she muttered as he turned to go. She pushed open the door, and he was right behind her, following her into the room.

"Don't go back there," he said in a curt tone.

"Why not? Roy and Danny are probably still there." She tried to recall the name of the tall, dark-haired cowboy... Jim? No, Jay. "Maybe someone will show me how to play pool." She stepped back, and he advanced. "I thought you were leaving."

"Grace." He captured her hand. "Promise me you won't go back there tonight." Something flared in his eyes, something dark and intense. Something that excited her.

She tipped her head back. "Why should I?"

"Because I'm asking."

It almost worked. She was so mesmerized by his hazel eyes that she nearly gave in to him. "Oh, please. Just go."

He caught her chin as she turned away and gently brought her face back to his. "We want the same thing. Just not like this."

"Like what?" she asked cautiously, not convinced they were thinking along the same lines. Then it registered. "You do think I'm drunk."

"No," he said, shaking his head, a trace of hesitation in his voice. "I don't."

"Tipsy?"

"Yes." He brushed the hair away from her eyes. "No crime in that."

"I drank two beers in two hours. I'm relaxed. That's all." She closed her eyes, enjoying his gentle touch, melting as his fingers moved to her scalp. "Just so you know... I decided when I got your text."

He stopped massaging. Let silence stretch until it almost snapped. "Decided what?"

She lifted her lashes. "Stay and I'll show you."

Ben's quick inhale held no warning.

His lips came down on hers. She opened her mouth, and he swept his tongue inside with an urgency that left her breathless. He moved his hands to her shoulders, then ran his palms down her arms. The feel and scent of his warm skin blurred her senses. She leaned against his hard chest, shivering when he closed his hands around her wrists.

His sudden and swift withdrawal caused her to stumble. He held her away from him until she'd secured her footing, then released her.

"Not now," he said, his voice harsh.

Harsh enough to make her wince. She had to resist the impulse to cross her arms over her chest. Hide her tightened nipples. Abrupt as he might be now, he'd been aroused only a moment ago.

"Look, I have someplace I need to be." He couldn't quite meet her eyes. "We'll talk tomorrow."

Too embarrassed, too confused by what had just happened, she said nothing. She simply watched Ben walk away, out the door, leaving her alone and humiliated.

BEN STOOD OUTSIDE The Watering Hole, trying to regain his composure. The bar was about the last place he wanted to be, but he had to do this for Grace's sake. He owed her this much after nearly giving in and taking her to bed. Oh yeah, he wanted her all right. But not when her judgment was the slightest impaired. Or while everyone in the bar assumed he'd spent the night with her.

The moment he stepped inside, he realized that showing up was the easy part. Stopping himself from slamming Roy and Danny against the wall—now that tested his self-control.

He spotted a vacant stool at the end of the bar and headed straight for it without glancing in the deputies' direction. But he knew they were still there.

A minute later, Sadie appeared in front of him, eyebrows drawn. "Didn't expect to see you back here. I sure hope you're not planning on busting up my place."

Slowly, he unclenched his jaw. "Now why would you say that?"

"I've been tending this bar for over thirty years. I know trouble when I see it. You're pissed off about something."

He smiled, not bothering to deny it. "I won't start anything. You have my word. How about another whiskey?"

Still frowning, she grabbed the Jack Daniel's off the shelf. "Just remember, you so much as break a glass or throw a punch and you won't be welcome back here. That's my number one rule, and it goes for everybody. No exceptions."

"I understand."

Without taking her eyes off his face, she free-poured him a perfect shot. "This have anything to do with Roy and Danny?"

He reached for the glass, paused, then picked it up. He'd sure hate it if Sadie had known what was going on without putting a stop to it. "Did you know what they were doing?"

"Not for certain. After you left, Gretchen told me something mighty disturbing. I was hoping she'd misread the situation."

Ben tossed back the whiskey, savored the burn. "They were spiking Grace's beer."

"Dumb bastards." Sadie glared at the deputies. "Gotta say I'm surprised at both of them, but Roy especially. Wade must be rubbing off on him." Her frown deepened. "I bet Grace could press charges if she wanted. Not that I can see her doing that."

"Grace doesn't know, and I'd like it to stay that way. At least for now."

Sadie nodded at the door. "Well, speak of the devil."

Without being obvious, Ben turned just enough to see who she meant. Wearing a uniform shirt that was too big for his thin frame, Wade sauntered in as if he owned the place. He stopped to shake hands with a table of old-timers. Likely already campaigning for the sheriff's job.

Ben faced Sadie again before Wade saw him. "Is he on duty?"

"Yep. He's walking over to Roy and Danny. I'll bet you dollars to doughnuts it was Wade who put those boys up to that mischief." A young cowboy at the other end of the bar called for a beer, and she nodded at him.

She poured more Jack Daniel's in Ben's glass before grabbing a mug and filling it from the tap.

Keeping his head down, Ben reminded himself he

wouldn't let his temper get the best of him. He'd already done what he'd set out to do. Those guys had seen him. They knew he'd walked Grace out and that was it. Tomorrow, after he cooled off, he'd have a talk with them. All he needed to do now was get square with Sadie and blow out of town for a while. Maybe head to Kalispell. Burn off some energy and frustration.

"Ben. Ben Carter, you ol' son-of-a-gun."

He didn't recognize the voice coming from over his right shoulder, but he could guess. He swiveled slowly around. Ignoring Wade's extended hand, Ben leaned back, propping his elbows on the bar. "You must be Wade."

"Come on, you're messing with me." Wade glanced at the guy sitting a stool over, then rested his hand on the butt of his holstered Glock. "You really don't remember me?" he murmured in a low, offended voice.

"It might be coming back to me."

"I was a grade behind you in school. We played football together."

Ben made sure his smile left no doubt that he remembered Wade as a benchwarmer. "So what are you up to these days, besides playing deputy?"

Wade still had the same nervous tic in his jaw. "Not for long. You probably heard Noah's leaving." He hooked his thumbs in his gun belt and squared his shoulders. "I'm next in line to be sheriff."

"Won't that be decided by vote?"

He snorted. "It's a no-brainer." Wade glanced at the two deputies sitting at the table. He leaned closer and said, "Between you and me, Roy's not ready. Danny's too young and one shy of a six-pack. Gus is already semiretired. He only works part-time to get away from his wife."

"What about Grace?" Ben asked with deceptive calm. "Did you forget about her?"

"Hell, who's gonna want a woman sheriff? Nah, she won't last long here." Wade propped a boot on the rail running along the foot of the bar, settling in, making it seem as if they were old friends catching up. "What are you doing sitting here, anyway? Here I had the boys get her all primed and ready for you. She get too sloppy for you, bro?"

Ben's blood pressure surged. "So you told them to spike her beer with shots."

For a lawman, Wade's instincts weren't worth a damn. The dumb bastard grinned. "Of course, I know you got your pick of all those hot Hollywood babes, but I figured Grace isn't so bad. She'd do in a—" He met Ben's eyes and paled.

"The only reason I haven't laid you out cold is because I promised Sadie I wouldn't cause any trouble." Ben shifted, and Wade jerked back. "If I were you, Deputy, I'd climb in your truck right now. As for your buddies…" he said with a small, controlled nod "…they might want to get a head start home before I finish my drink."

Wade's boots seemed frozen to the floor. He studied Ben a moment and then said, "I hope you didn't mean that as a threat."

Ben just smiled.

"I'll remind you we're all officers of the law," Wade muttered, his voice hoarse. "If I misunderstood you, no hard feelings."

"Let me make it real clear. I wouldn't lose a minute's sleep putting any one of you in the hospital."

Wade's fingers clenched around his gun like he was getting ready to whip it out, but Ben knew a coward when he saw one. Taking a step back, Wade glanced around, saw that no one was listening. "You watch yourself, son…" After another scowl, he turned tail, briefly stopping at Roy and Danny's table. Then he was out the door. The other two hurried shortly behind him.

"Better not be running out on your tab," Sadie called to them from behind the bar, then chuckled.

She could see as well as Ben that they'd left a wad of

cash on the table in their haste to leave. Ben didn't smile. No use stirring up everyone's curiosity. He'd purposely kept the conversation with Wade low and private. Not to save the man from embarrassment. He didn't give a shit about Wade. Ben wanted to spare Grace.

So he kept his mouth shut and pretended he was just enjoying a drink, then dug into his pocket for money.

After filling a pitcher for the waitress, Sadie returned with the bottle of Jack Daniel's. "Hell, if I'd known you wanted to tune Wade up a bit, I might've overlooked my no-fighting rule."

Ben stopped her when she tried to pour him more whiskey. "That's enough for me."

"You're not going after them," Sadie said when he laid a large bill on the bar. It wasn't a question.

He shook his head.

"You kick up a fuss and it'll come back on Grace."

"I know."

Her gaze sharpened. "Now it makes sense why you came back here," she said, her eyes warming with approval. "That was a kind thing you did. Around here, tongues wag about nothing. Grace doesn't need that kind of gossip."

"No woman does." He slid off the stool and checked his watch. He nixed the idea of driving to Kalispell. He was keyed up and feeling the effects of the liquor. Probably could use some food in his belly.

"Wait. Take your money."

"Keep it," he said, pausing to stretch a kink out of his neck. He needed a good workout. He rarely let three days go by without one.

"Ben?"

He was tempted to keep walking to the door. For whatever reason, he had a feeling Sadie was about to say something he wouldn't like. Out of politeness, he looked at her.

"You're a good man, Ben. Your mama must be mighty proud."

Ben bit back a curse. Sadie was dead wrong. If his mom was so proud of him, she would've trusted him with the truth.

9

LATE THE NEXT MORNING, Grace walked a jittery couple and their two kids out of the Sheriff's office and promised she'd call them with an update. Understandably, they were still upset. While camping in the foothills, they'd been awoken by gunfire. It wasn't hunting season. Grace and the father agreed that the shots might have come from poachers. Not aimed at the family, but the situation was still dangerous.

She stared at the schedule board, trying to decide how to proceed. For two weeks, it had been nice and quiet. Figured she'd be alone for the first serious incident report. She had no problem jumping in. She just wished she knew the area better. The campers were from Butte and hadn't been much help narrowing the location of the shots. Though from their description, she suspected they'd been fired above Weaver's Ridge.

Noah wouldn't return until evening. Roy's shift started in an hour. Danny was off and Wade had the swing shift. Gus was a mystery. She never could figure out his hours. Much as she hated bothering Roy, she called him. If it were her, she'd want to know what she was walking into.

"Roy, it's Grace," she said when he answered. "Got a minute?"

"What do you need?" he asked, his voice tentative. Was he annoyed because she'd left early last night?

"Sorry to call you at home, but campers reported shots being fired in the foothills. It's a family. They aren't local, so they gave me a vague location."

"Oh, okay. Probably poachers," he said, sounding oddly relieved.

She hoped that didn't mean he'd take the incident lightly. "That's what I'm thinking since no BOLOs were issued from other counties." Grace paused, but decided he must know the term meant to *be on the lookout.* "No reason to believe someone is hiding out up there. But according to the mother, the shots were close enough to their campsite that one of them could've been hit."

Roy snorted. "She all hysterical over it? What did the husband think?"

"They had two kids with them, Roy," Grace said, hanging on to her temper. "They had every right to be concerned."

"Yeah, okay. So what do you want from me?"

She frowned at his reaction, though, should she be surprised? While she wasn't looking to have her hand held, if the situation were reversed, she would've been out the door already to assist him. "Where's the best place for me to start looking and for us to meet up?"

After a long pause, he said, "Are you kidding me?"

She lifted the truck keys off the wall hook, hoping this conversation wasn't going the way she feared. "Your shift starts soon. No point in you coming to the office first."

"Don't go after them. That's crazy. Whether they're poachers or not, those guys have to be long gone by now."

"And if they just robbed a bank?"

"That's a lot of territory to cover."

"So basically you're saying we don't care about poachers or criminals in general. They have a free pass in Salina

County because the sheriff's department isn't willing to get off their asses."

"Ah, hell." Roy sighed. "Don't go getting in a snit. If Noah were here or we had another man on duty, we could've set up checkpoints on the highway to catch them when they came down. But your campers likely spooked them and they took off."

A snit? She really had to let that one go. For now. She privately admitted the checkpoints made sense. But that wasn't an option at the moment. "Mr. Anderson thought the shots came from a distance. From his description, I think he meant Weaver's Ridge. And isn't April a weird month to go camping? It's still cold at night, so if our perps are poachers, they probably didn't expect anyone else to be up there."

"Perps?" Roy snorted. "You ain't in the city anymore, Deputy Dawg."

Yeah, no kidding. Sighing, she rubbed her left temple. "Can we get back to the case?"

"Case? We have no case. Grace, I'm telling you to forget it. Let's just figure the shots were fired on BLM land— that's Bureau of Land Management."

"I know what it means, Roy," she said, her patience strained.

"Well, then call Fish and Wildlife. Let them worry about it."

"Is that what Noah would do?"

After a long, awkward moment, Roy said, "You wanna be stubborn? Then you're going up there by yourself."

She glanced at the large area map taped to the back wall. "Thanks," she murmured and hung up. If Roy wasn't willing to search the foothills, the others wouldn't join her.

Peering at the map, she spotted Weaver's Ridge. Nikki had mentioned that she and Trace were fixing up a house somewhere near there, so Grace had a vague notion of the area. And hadn't Ben said something about...

Oh, no. She squashed the thought. Even thinking about him was off-limits. She'd spent too much time fighting humiliation over his rejection last night. And then he'd lied about having someplace to go, probably to avoid hurting her feelings, but that didn't help. According to a nice older rancher who'd been eating his eggs and bacon at the diner when she'd stopped for a cinnamon roll, Ben had returned to The Watering Hole. If Ben had found some company, Clyde hadn't said.

She removed her Glock from the drawer and holstered it. She checked the ammo in the Remington and grabbed extra magazines. Ideally, her cell phone would work, though she knew there were pockets where service was spotty. She'd have to rely on the radio if she needed help. And she prayed Roy would be around to answer.

HALFWAY TO THE SUNDANCE, Ben turned on the Porsche's air conditioner. He was starting to sweat, both literally and figuratively. And because of two different women, of all the damn things. Lena still hadn't returned his calls. And then Grace—hell, he couldn't figure out why she was getting under his skin.

Rachel's friends had left the ranch, and with things still unsettled with his mom, Ben had decided to stick around for the rest of the week. It made sense to move to the Sundance. But with Grace staying in the room next to his, he wasn't going anywhere.

Last night had been a waste. After leaving The Watering Hole, twice he'd found himself about to knock on Grace's door. He wasn't clear on what held him back. He'd never turned down a tipsy woman before. He wasn't that noble. Her inhibitions might be dulled, but she still knew what she was doing. A drunk woman? Different story.

What was it about Grace that had him acting like Sir Friggin' Galahad? What brought out the protective instinct that was so foreign to him it made the back of his neck itch? Funny, because she wasn't the type who needed him or anyone else to defend her. But something about her calm self-assurance got to him in a way he found hard to explain.

The pull was almost primitive, in his DNA, a part of his biological makeup. He could've hooked up with several different women at the wedding who were usually— physically, at least—more to his liking.

His thoughts returned to Lena. She was older and still a pretty wild player, attracting men of all ages. But he'd never regretted his decision to keep sex out of their relationship. She had enough playthings. The two of them were friends, and he was her plus-one when she needed him.

Everything had always worked fine between them, but now? Not returning his calls? Screw the fun and games. This was business. Buying the ranch was his only goal. Meanwhile, she had her red-tipped talons in many different pots. He wanted some distance from Hollywood, to live away from the phony smiles and toxic relationships. Not that he didn't want the Hollywood money, but with the ranch, he'd mostly be dealing with the wranglers he'd gotten to know over the years. People who worked with the animals during filming and knew him well enough to expect good stock and trained horses from him.

Sure, he'd still be on set sometimes, but only because he wanted to be. In truth, he'd probably have to do stunt work for a time, but man, he could practically see the barns and corrals filled with prime stock.

He'd been deep into the party life before, but not for a while now. If he'd harbored a doubt or two about changing careers, coming home had helped sort him out.

Home.

The unconscious thought didn't sit well. No use getting sentimental now. Montana, the Sundance, none of it had been home for a long time. His friends were in LA. His job. His ranch was in Ventura. Or would be soon. In a matter of days, the deal would be done. And he might not have the Rockies to look at from his front porch, but the beach wasn't too far. And with Ojai and the Los Padres National Forest a short drive away, he wouldn't be hurting for beautiful scenery.

The minute he turned down the gravel road to the Sundance, he called the bank to get a status on the loan. He wasn't worried about it, not really, the bank president was a personal friend of Lena's and she had millions invested through Judd Hinton. But since Ben couldn't talk to her, he hoped hearing *something* would blunt his edginess.

He had Hinton's assistant on speed dial. She was a woman in her midforties. Smart, efficient, always well dressed, and she always blushed when he teased her. "Janice, it's Ben Wolf."

"Ben." She paused. "Are you back in town?"

"Why? You miss me?"

Her laugh was brief and nervous. "Mr. Hinton isn't here at the moment."

"I don't need to speak to him." Something was wrong. She never went straight to business like that. "Have you got the final loan documents ready for our signatures?"

"No, I'm afraid I don't."

"Is there a holdup?"

Her resigned sigh knotted his insides. "I might as well tell you…Ben, the loan's been denied."

"That's not possible."

"I don't know what else to say."

"Tell me you're joking." He waited a moment that seemed like an eternity. "How can that be? Lena has all kinds of— Where's Hinton? I need to speak to him."

"He's not in his office," Janice said, which Ben didn't believe. "Speaking to him won't do any good. Look, you'll find out anyway. Ms. Graves withdrew the loan request."

"She did what?" He was coming up on the Sundance. Cole was waiting to show him a pair of colts he thought

Ben might want. "There must be a mistake. Lena's been on board from the beginning..."

"I have to go. I'm late for a meeting."

"Wait. What if I carry the loan? I can come up with some of the down payment. Would fifteen percent work?" His desperate plea was met with silence. "Janice?"

"I'm sorry, Ben. I really am." The sympathy in her voice angered him. "There's nothing I can do."

Feeling the rage building, Ben bit off a curse. "I understand," he murmured, then disconnected before he said something he'd regret.

He drove the last stretch to the Sundance, not giving one damn about his speed, and parked under the cottonwood tree, trying like hell to calm himself. Cole had already seen him. If he hadn't been standing outside the barn, Ben would've considered turning around and driving straight to LA.

What had he been thinking? Hadn't he learned anything? From the lies he'd been fed as a kid to the lies he'd lived with in the backstabbing capital of the West Coast, he should have known something would go wrong the minute he was out of town.

So what the hell was he supposed to do now? Here he'd gotten Cole's hopes up about them doing business together.

Shit.

Ben slammed his palm against the dashboard. Not hard enough. He slammed it again. Who was he fooling? He was thinking more about himself than the McAllisters. He'd come with his chest puffed out, driving his flashy car, showing off, the guy no one thought would amount to anything. Once he'd seen the condition of the Sundance, he'd wanted to help. And yeah, he'd gotten off on knowing they needed him.

If he couldn't come through, he was going to look like a goddamn ass. Or he could tell Cole his partner already found a stock supplier. Just to save face.

Damn Lena. They'd drawn up a business plan, crunched numbers and even projected when to expect a profit. This venture wasn't charity. She had most of the money and financial connections, and Ben had the expertise and the contacts to place the animals for top dollar. This was supposed to be a fifty/fifty partnership. And now she was treating him like a toy she'd grown tired of by not returning his calls? And pulling this bullshit with the loan?

Cole was frowning, so Ben got out of the car while trying to sort out his jumbled thoughts. He needed to keep his cool. No sense telling Cole anything yet. This wasn't over. Ben would talk to Lena, and he knew just how to get her attention. If she wanted to play dirty, he was happy to oblige her.

Ben had just about reached Cole when he heard a vehicle coming up behind him. It was a sheriff's department truck. And speaking of beautiful women creating havoc, Grace was driving.

Grace spotted the Porsche and held her breath as embarrassment crashed over her. Now wasn't the time to let a personal problem distract her from what she had to do. So Ben had rejected her last night. She was a big girl. She'd get over it. But damn it, why did she have to see him now?

Cole smiled as she approached.

Ben gave her a blank look.

"Afternoon, Grace." Cole pushed up the brim of his hat. "What brings you out here?"

Keeping her expression neutral, she nodded at Ben. He barely acknowledged her. "I was hoping Trace was around."

"He's in Missoula. Won't be back until late tonight. Anything I can help you with?"

Damn. "Marge at the diner suggested I talk to him." Grace spotted a hawk and watched it soar toward the Big Belt Mountains. Beautiful country and a whole lot of it.

A person could easily get lost. "I'm trying to figure out which is the best way to cross Weaver's Ridge."

"Yeah." Cole nodded, rueful. "Trace is your man. He knows the place like the back of his hand." He glanced at Ben. "You remember the area? Isn't that where you and Trace used to go fishing?"

Ben stared at Cole as if he were speaking a different language. He seemed preoccupied and clearly hadn't been following the conversation.

Cole eyed him a moment, then looked at her. "You asking for business or pleasure?"

"I wish it were pleasure," she said. "A family camping up there reported gunshots. I'm thinking poachers."

Cole frowned. "Anyone get hurt?"

"No. The mom and kids were shaken up, but that's it."

Cole glanced thoughtfully at her truck. "Even four-wheel drive won't take you far," he said. "At some point, you'd have to go on foot. Horseback might be the best option."

"Same goes for the poachers, then. They must've parked ATVs somewhere."

"You don't know for sure you're dealing with poachers." Cole squinted at the mountains.

"No, but it makes sense." She didn't like the growing concern on his face. "Any militia groups around here?"

"Not that I'm aware of." He shrugged. "You're probably right about them being poachers. Any idea if they knew about the campers?"

"Hard to say. Apparently, the woman screamed, but the husband was adamant the shots were fired from a distance so they might not have heard her." Grace checked her watch. "I have to get moving—"

"I hope you're not thinking of going up by yourself. Those foothills can be tricky if you're not familiar with the area." Cole shot another look at Ben.

Unable to stop herself, she glanced at him, too. He

stared into the distance, seeming miles away. Maybe his brooding had nothing to do with her or last night. One thing for sure, he wasn't just distracted. He was in a hell of a bad mood.

"Well, thanks," she said, backing away. "I really appreciate the information." The last thing she wanted was for him or Cole to think she was asking for help to do her job.

"Wait." Ben's gruff tone made her more tense. "Cole's right. Most trails dead-end, and the rest can get you lost. Don't go up there alone."

Yes, sir. She resisted the impulse to salute him and his high-handed decree. "Roy comes on duty in thirty minutes." It wasn't a lie. If Ben assumed she was waiting for backup, that was his problem.

"Great," he said with a snort of disgust. "I'm sure the stupid bastard will be a big help."

Cole gave him a stunned look.

Grace refused to engage. "Thanks again," she said and hurried to the truck, wishing she hadn't wasted the time driving to the Sundance. Yeah, she'd half hoped Trace would've gone with her had he been there. She was pretty good at tracking, but not knowing her way around the area was a handicap. And no telling how many perps she'd be facing.

Maybe Roy was right. Maybe searching the foothills was foolish. But it was also her job. And she hadn't given up everything she loved in Arizona to bungle a chance to take back her life and save her career.

10

By THE TIME Ben left the Sundance, he thought seriously about going back to bed and starting the day over. Except he couldn't turn off his brain. His anger at Lena was eating at him. He hadn't clarified yesterday's conversation with his mother yet. And what was he supposed to tell Cole about the pair of colts he was saving for him?

If all that crap wasn't enough, thoughts of Grace kept sneaking in to confuse him further. Much as he resented returning to LA without getting to know her better, he had little choice but to leave today. Tomorrow morning at the latest. He had to either get to Lena and talk some sense into her or start liquidating his assets. If he even had enough to qualify for the loan. He'd hate giving up the Porsche. But if that's what it took to buy the ranch, so be it.

Five miles outside of town, he called Grace and was sent straight to voice mail. He figured she was probably with Roy. Ben doubted the guy had been gung ho about climbing those hills and had talked her out of the search. With the nightly rain showers, the place was bound to be muddy. Terrific for tracking, terrible for everything else. More than likely, the shooters had disappeared before the campers even made it to town.

It was already getting late, and he needed to decide soon

if it was worth driving to LA tonight. One thing lifted his mood. He'd left messages for Lena with three of her friends. He smiled. She was going to flip out. Especially if Tricia got to her first. The woman was more frenemy than friend and lived and breathed gossip. She'd tried baiting him for more information, but he'd played dumb. Lena would hate everyone knowing she was avoiding him. Ben couldn't have cared less.

He pulled onto Main Street and glanced at the dashboard clock, not surprised that he hadn't received a call yet. It was Lena's spa day, so she wouldn't be glued to her phone. He drove past The Boarding House and spotted a white sheriff's truck parked in front of the office.

As he got closer, he saw that it was Roy leaning against the passenger door. He was talking to Wade and Danny, neither of them wearing a uniform shirt. Grace was probably inside writing a report.

He parked the Porsche and got out. The men were laughing until Danny spotted him. He said something to the other two who instantly shut up. Wade hooked his thumbs in his jeans as Ben approached. The other two started twitching like a pair of virgins hoping to get laid.

The truck was nice and clean, even the tires. No trace of mud. "Is Grace inside?"

Roy averted his gaze.

Danny flushed red, mumbling something about having to go home, then hurried down the sidewalk.

Ben's stomach clenched. No, he had to be misreading the situation. They might be pricks, but they wouldn't let her go up to Weaver's Ridge by herself. He stared at Wade, daring the man to weasel out of an answer. "Where is she, Wade? Where's Grace?"

"How should I know?" The tic had started in his jaw, and he fleetingly met Ben's eyes. "I'm not even on duty yet."

"You wouldn't be lying to me, would you, Wade?"

"She's not here," Roy said, his voice cracking. "She might've gone to Weaver's Ridge."

Ben glared at Roy.

"I told her not to go," the deputy said. "I did. Ask her. I flat-out told her we would set up checkpoints if we had the manpower, but not search on foot. Not for poachers."

Ben couldn't speak. Fury ripped through him. Underneath it was fear. Fear that something could have happened to Grace. Fear that he wouldn't be able to gain control of himself. He couldn't give in to the rage. It would cripple him.

"Have you had contact with her?" Ben hit speed dial. "The radio…can you reach her?" he asked, then cursed when he got her voice mail.

"I've tried." Roy shook his head. "I even drove up to see which trail she used," he said, darting a glance at Wade. "It's good and muddy, but I didn't see tire tracks."

"Come on, she didn't go up there," Wade said. "She's probably found someplace off the highway where she can read a magazine."

Ben stared at him in utter disbelief. "You stupid bastard. I met her three days ago and even I know her better than that."

"He's right," Roy muttered. "She's got a stubborn streak in her."

Ben shook his head. "Grace isn't afraid to do her job." He ducked his head inside the cab of the truck and grabbed the rifle mounted in back.

"Hey, what are you doing?" Wade said. "That's county property. You can't touch that."

Behind the seat, Ben found a box of bullets. He straightened and looked from Wade to Roy. "Either of you wanna try and stop me?"

Wade glared back, but didn't move.

Roy hung his head.

"That's what I thought," Ben said, giving Wade a cocky smile before heading for the Porsche.

"I'm coming with you." Roy hustled around the truck to the driver's door.

"You can't keep up." Ben wasn't about to sugarcoat things. "Keep trying the radio. If you get through, tell her I'll be right behind her."

GRACE HEARD ANOTHER shot and ducked, using the tree for cover. It was an automatic reflex. She was fairly certain the shooter wasn't close. It sounded as though the shot had come from the direction of the neighboring ridge, but it was difficult to gauge. She moved out into the open and scanned the mountainside, hoping to see something—sunlight glinting off a rifle barrel, movement, a color that didn't belong—anything that would point her in the right direction.

The birds were quiet. Insects had stopped chirping. Even the breeze no longer rustled the leaves. She shuddered at the unnatural silence. And then she heard it. Behind her, a twig snapped, and dead leaves crunched under footfalls. She froze.

"It's just me, Grace." Ben's low voice nearly gave her a heart attack.

She spun around, gulping in air, her gaze flying to the rifle in his hand. "What are you doing here?"

"Same as you," he said with a peculiarly sweet smile, then turned his head and peered at the ridge. "Sounded like the shot came from over there."

"I think so." She slid him another look, just to make sure he wasn't a hallucination.

He stayed focused on the tree line. "Gotta admit, I'm surprised the idiots are still around."

"Obviously, they didn't know about the campers."

"The weather's been warm. They should've figured they might not be up here alone. You find anything yet?"

"A young doe," Grace said, controlling a shudder at the senseless killing. Hunting for food was one thing, but she'd never understood hunting for sport or trophies. "Two shots. They didn't take anything."

"No, they're looking for a buck. They want antlers. So now you know they're most likely poachers." He squinted up at the late afternoon sun. "Bad time of day to hunt, though."

"No one said they were smart." She drew in more air. Wow, had she underestimated the effects of the altitude. "They could be kids, stupid, drunk or all of the above."

"Anyone who grew up around here knows better." Ben continued to scan the ridge. "Could be tourists hoping to take back a souvenir," he said grimly.

"How did you find me?" she asked, willing to admit she was glad to see him. There'd been no cell service for two hours, and her radio was on its last leg.

"The same way you found them." He nodded at the boot prints in the soft ground. "You figure out how many there are?"

"I believe three. The family who reported the shots used the trail that forked off a mile back. The kids' prints made them easy to distinguish." A buzzing insect landed on her arm, and she slapped it. Her skin was covered with welts and scrapes. She hadn't noticed until now.

Apparently, so did Ben. His gaze lingered on a particularly nasty gash.

She turned to continue on the trail at the same time her radio emitted a burst of static. She left the volume turned down, but listened closely. Still nothing.

"Have you talked to Roy?"

"Not since this morning." She gave the radio a light whack. "Why?"

"I asked him to let you know I was on my way."

She eyed the Remington. "Is that a department rifle?"

An excited yelp echoed off the ridge, followed by whoops of laughter.

She and Ben looked at each other. They both knew the celebration meant the last shot had resulted in a kill. Her stomach lurched.

"I know this area," Ben said, his gaze skimming the stain on her jeans from when she'd slipped on a slimy creek bottom. "They sound closer than they are. You should consider turning this over to Fish and Wildlife."

"But we're here and we have a better chance—"

"No, we don't. Grace." He caught her hand, making sure he had her attention before releasing her. "We're not going to gain on them. It's likely they have four-wheelers waiting on the other side. We're on government land. You have to notify Fish and Wildlife, anyway."

She knew he was right. The BLM had jurisdiction and the proper staff to go after poachers. But still, returning empty-handed was going to be hard...a blow to her pride. If only she could've moved faster. The high altitude was no excuse. She'd always been strong and disciplined. But since moving to Blackfoot Falls...

"I guess Roy was right." She sighed, too exhausted to care. All she wanted was to get back to the truck. "This was a colossal waste of time."

"The hell it was. You had no way of knowing where this would lead. You're doing your job, even though it would've been easy to let it go. Just ask the three idiots loitering outside the Sheriff's office."

She gave him a mock glare. "You didn't give them a hard time, did you?"

"Now, why would I do that?" he said, his tone and expression bland. Which made her laugh. Ben smiled. Then his eyes narrowed on her arm. He touched the bruised skin, his fingers gentle, but she flinched anyway. "Maybe I *should* go after the bastards," he murmured.

His quiet, emotionless voice worried her.

"No one's going after them," she said. "You just convinced me not to. Come on, let's head back."

Ben seemed fixated on her arm, but he finally nodded. "You need to clean out that gash right away. I assume you have a first aid kit in the truck."

She sighed. The scrape was nothing. She'd wait until she returned to the office. After a final look back at the ridge, Grace led him to the trail that would take them to the creek where she'd nearly fallen on her butt. From there, she estimated it would be another four miles to the truck.

They walked in silence. She noticed the birds were singing again, and unfortunately, the flying insects who found her fair skin a delicacy had returned to feast. She swatted at them, but even that seemed like too much effort. She was tired, grimy and sweaty, and she sure wasn't smelling like a rose.

"You want to rest a few minutes?" Ben asked as they approached the creek.

"I'm good," she said, torn between taking a breather and hurrying back to a hot shower. "You need to stop?"

"I could use a break."

"Liar." She could see a smile lurking at the corners of his mouth. "You aren't even winded."

"Look, the altitude gets to everybody. Blackfoot Falls is just over sixty-eight hundred feet. Tack on another fifteen hundred where we are now."

"At least we're going downhill." She eyed the pair of large, flat rocks poking out of the water. "Those are not stepping stones. Avoid them like the plague."

He tested another rock with the toe of his boot. His very expensive-looking boot that was now caked with mud and probably ruined.

"Why didn't you change your boots?" she asked, and accepted the hand he offered as they crossed the creek.

"I didn't think about it." He glanced down and winced.

"I saw Wade and the other two outside the office and knew you were alone up here. Noah ought to fire their asses."

Grace's heart fluttered. "That was really nice of you. To worry about me. Unnecessary, but still—" For God's sake, she was babbling. Proof she was tired. She let go of his hand and concentrated on where she was stepping. "I owe you a new pair of boots."

"Nope."

"It's the least I can do."

"Dinner," he said, and checked his phone. "Tonight."

She stopped to dig for hers. "Do you have cell service?"

"Not yet." He was practically glaring at his phone. She could almost see the same dark cloud from this morning descending on him. "Are you off duty after you get back?"

"I'll have to make the call to Fish and Wildlife," she said, already dreading it. "And write a report."

"That shouldn't take long."

"Yeah," she murmured, disgusted. "Not much to tell."

"Hey, you did your badge proud today. And that's something coming from me. I don't even like cops."

Grace laughed. "Gee, thanks."

"I've met too many like Roy and Wade."

"Roy really isn't so bad."

Ben's mouth tightened. Clearly, he disagreed. He started to say something but then let it go. Which she appreciated, because she wasn't about to expend energy defending Roy.

"When you call Fish and Wildlife, tell the warden you think the poachers came up the ridge from Maryville. That's a damn good guess since we know they didn't park vehicles on this side."

"Thanks. That's good information, though it won't matter this time. They'll be long gone. My fault for not giving the Wildlife people a heads-up."

"Quit feeling sorry for yourself, Deputy. It doesn't suit you."

Grace shot him a dirty look. The amusement in his face

irritated the hell out of her. "I am not feeling sorry for myself. I'm taking responsibility for screwing up."

"My mistake," he said with a faint smirk. "I don't know if you've dealt with poachers before, but they're rarely caught in the act. Those guys like to brag. I guarantee you they end up at a bar getting drunk and shooting off their mouths. That's how they'll get caught."

"See, there's the problem. If only you'd told me you were an expert on the subject, it would've saved me a lot of hassle."

Ben laughed. "Don't get huffy and think you're getting out of dinner."

Ignoring him, she continued down the trail, wincing when tree branches grazed her scraped arms. She couldn't think about dinner or make the leap to what might happen afterward. It wouldn't surprise her if her whole body ended up one giant welt. If nothing else, today served as a valuable lesson. Working outdoors in northern Montana held different challenges than the Arizona desert, and she needed to be better prepared.

Her head wasn't in the game. It humbled her to admit she'd dismissed Blackfoot Falls as a hick town that was beneath her instead of familiarizing herself with her new surroundings. Because she'd been too preoccupied with the guy who'd climbed a mountain to have her back. A guy who was leaving in a couple of days. And now she'd botched her first case.

She was smarter than that, damn it.

11

BEN STRIPPED OFF his muddy boots and clothes. He'd never stayed in a place with a worse shower. The stall was too small, the pressure barely adequate. He had to duck to get under the spray. But all he felt was grateful when the hot water sluiced down his back. Poor Grace, with her scrapes and cuts, had gone straight to the Sheriff's office to notify Fish and Wildlife and write her report. She hadn't complained once. Hadn't given Roy or Wade so much as a dirty look. Ben had no doubt she'd keep them out of the report.

He crouched, leaning his hand against the shower wall to let the water pelt his neck while he took deep breaths, trying to rid himself of the urge to bloody a few noses. That was progress. Thirty minutes ago, he'd been ready to do a lot more damage to the three deputies.

With a single look, Grace had made him back off. He'd been angry at the time, but he quickly realized how right she'd been. God, she was really something. Strong, controlled, capable, so damn independent. She had more integrity and courage than Wade, Roy and Danny put together. It would've been an insult to her if Ben had tried to intercede.

He hoped she'd finished up by now and was in her room, but he doubted it. He'd left her right after she'd called Fish and Wildlife. He'd wanted to walk her back to the inn, but she'd sent him on his way.

Just as well. She wouldn't want to eat dinner out. He knew that much. While she showered, he'd pick up something at the diner or Food Mart and bring it to the room. In fact, he preferred they had some private time. Even if it turned out they just ate.

Not his first choice, but she was exhausted. He'd seen it in her face and the stiff way she had moved. She needed rest, and he wasn't going anywhere. At least not tonight. Tomorrow he'd reevaluate his options. Lena hadn't called yet, but she would.

Oddly, he'd managed to forget about her, about the loan, about the whole damn mess. And even the thing yesterday with his mom. His entire focus had been on Grace.

He turned off the water and grabbed a towel from the rack. This morning, he hadn't managed more than five minutes alone with his mom. First, they'd been interrupted by Cole and some of the ranch hands, and then again by Rachel, who'd wanted the recipe for tortilla soup.

Considering his lousy mood over the loan, it was probably for the best. He needed to talk with Claudia first before confronting their mom. Nine years ago, his contact with her had been limited, so Claudia had passed on the news of their father's death. By then, Ben had quit asking questions. He'd been filming on location in Mexico the day his sister had called to tell him. He remembered getting stinking drunk on tequila afterward. And paid hell for it the next day.

While he finished drying off, he mulled over how he'd approach the issue. On the drive back from the Sundance, he'd left a voice mail for Claudia, who had a doctor's appointment and then some class or another. He'd wait for her, find out if he was wrong about the gap in their mother's story. Though his sister could be as blind as the McAllisters when it came to Hilda.

Why no one else seemed concerned that his own mother had lied to him about his father was beyond him. Even Claudia seemed fine with the situation. Well, that was their business, and he swore that the next time he saw his mother, he wasn't going to let it slide.

After tossing the damp towel in the bathroom, Ben wandered to the window and peered down Main Street toward the Sheriff's office, wondering if Grace was still there. She could be in her room already, but he wasn't going to bother her. Maybe she'd take his advice and catch a nap after she showered. Besides, he had dinner to figure out.

He let the drapes fall back into place, paused, and nearly yanked the right side off the rod trying to take another look. A woman in gray sweats was jogging toward the south end of town. Slender build, brown hair blazing with auburn highlights from the late afternoon sun. A woman who looked a hell of a lot like Grace.

He stretched his neck from side to side, settled on the edge of the bed, then stood again. The woman was Grace. What in hell was she doing going for a run after all the physical exertion of today? What was she trying to prove?

Had something else happened?

None of his damn business, now was it?

Theoretically, that was true. But he could feel the tension pulsing through him—frustration, edginess, all churning in the pit of his stomach. Left alone, nothing good would come of it.

"Screw it." He grabbed a pair of jeans.

Grace could do all the running she wanted.

After he left for LA.

TWENTY-FIVE MINUTES into a measly two-mile run, Grace was willing to admit she'd pushed too hard. After an exhausting afternoon and unused to the altitude, she was only punishing herself. And for what? Making bad decisions was becoming a real problem. It had been her choice to go after the poachers. She'd chosen to quit her job and leave Arizona. No one had forced her hand. Eventually, it might've come to that, once Internal Affairs officially closed the case on T.J.'s murder, but this move was her own doing.

Unless she got a job in a city with a larger and more progressive sheriff's department, there would always be guys like Wade and Roy who were threatened by a woman. Especially one whose qualifications were more impressive than their own.

She'd faced gender bias in Arizona—there'd been a couple of idiot deputies who'd tried to get under her skin. She hadn't let them, and she wouldn't let Wade, Roy, Danny or anybody else do it in Montana.

In fact, if she disregarded Clarence and her job situation, it wasn't so bad in Blackfoot Falls. If only she'd give the place a chance. She was on her way to being friends with Rachel, Nikki and Sadie. The whole McAllister clan had been terrific.

And there was Ben. But he'd be leaving soon, and that was a good thing. It couldn't go any other way for her. Not if she wanted to adjust to her new life, be happy. Even resigned and semicontent would work for her.

But Ben, with his deep, raspy voice and seductive eyes, his charming smile, his calm self-assurance...he wasn't just gorgeous—he was far more astute and controlled than the rumors gave him credit for. Oh, he'd been furious with Wade and Roy. The bloodlust in his eyes had been obvious. But he'd understood the fight was hers, and he'd backed off. She knew it hadn't been easy for him.

He had a tender side, too. Maybe even a bit of a hero complex. That made her smile, especially knowing he'd deny it to his dying breath. That he'd gone up the mountain after her still boggled her mind.

"It's just me, Grace."

His quiet words echoing in her head brought a lump to her throat.

He had no idea how much his support meant to her. No one besides her father had been in her corner for a very long time.

She wasn't about to fall apart over the small kindness. But heaven help the next person to make a negative comment about him. Including Clarence.

Ben might've been a troublemaker as a teenager, a kid people like her uncle believed would never amount to anything, but Ben had grown into a strong, thoughtful man.

The main problem with him was that he made her feel and want things she shouldn't. Peace and contentment—those should be her only goals.

But she couldn't do anything about her future tonight. She'd promised to have dinner with him, and she'd keep her word.

Winded and feeling overheated, she left the road and took refuge under the shade of a scrawny tree. It wasn't that warm, and she'd hydrated. The problem was, her body was no longer pumped full of adrenaline. She was simply exhausted, and the thought of having to walk back to town made her want to curl up into a ball.

She bent, stretching her leg muscles, and ordering herself not to pass out. The rocky ground was littered with dead branches and dry fall leaves, but she spotted a place to sit until she caught her breath. At the sound of an approaching car, she looked up with tentative hope. Catching a ride back would be great if it was someone who wasn't a deputy.

Of course it was a red Porsche. What the heck, right? He'd already seen her fail once today, so why not make it an even number? She moved away from the tree and closer to the road, wondering if he was headed to the Sundance or looking for her.

He cruised to a stop and lowered the passenger window. "And here I thought you were the smart deputy."

"Nice. Really smooth." She didn't wait for an invitation but opened the passenger door and slid onto the cool leather seat. "Great pickup line."

"It worked."

She'd walked right into that one. Didn't stop her from giving him a *look*. Seeing his faint grin, she laughed. "Just drive."

"Where are we going?"

"Back to town." She snuggled down, enjoying the cool blast of air coming from the vent.

He drove several feet, then veered toward the narrow shoulder. She expected him to make a U-turn. Instead, he stopped the Porsche.

She sat up and glanced around. "What are you doing?"

Ben slid an arm behind her, ignoring her startled squeak, and kissed her. On the mouth. Warm lips, no tongue. Demanding nothing. Giving more than taking.

A protest died in her throat. How could a chaste kiss feel this good? He'd found a nice, comfortable pressure that seemed to ease the day's tension. Even if she'd known ahead of time he was going to kiss her, she wouldn't have expected this.

He cupped her face, his rough palm gently cradling her cheek as he changed the slant of his mouth. This time, he wasn't quite so gentle. There was a bit more pressure now, and it was good. The minute the tip of his tongue touched the seam of her lips, she was a goner, opening to him on a sigh. Pressing closer, she tried to ignore the inconvenient console as she breathed in the scent of him.

It seemed as if the Porsche had suddenly shrunk. Frustrated, she shifted, trying to find a more satisfactory position. But it was no use.

With great reluctance, she broke the kiss. "Let's go, okay?"

Ben drew back, his darkened gaze lingering on her lips. "You still owe me dinner," he said and met her eyes.

"I know." She resettled in the leather seat, aware that he might be wondering whether she planned to ditch him.

"Something else you should know..." He slipped the car into gear. "I'm not letting you out of my sight."

Grace laughed softly. "I have to shower again."

Amusement gleamed in his eyes. "What's your point?"

FORTY-FIVE MINUTES LATER, hair slightly damp, Grace knocked on Ben's door. It was 7:00 p.m. on the nose, which had given her a chance to shower and to make up her mind about the night to come, and him time to gather his secret meal that she suspected was a secret only because he had no idea what to buy. She assumed it was a couple of boxed sandwiches from the Food Mart.

The second he opened the door, she smelled food. Roast chicken, if she wasn't mistaken. From the diner. It was one of her favorites.

He checked his watch. "Cutting it close."

She smiled sweetly. "Bite me," she said and crossed the threshold.

With a laugh, he caught her around the waist and closed the door with his foot.

"Stop it, you nutcase." Trying to pry his arm away was useless. "Assault on a deputy is a serious charge."

"You gonna report me?"

"Hell, no. I'll arrest you myself."

"Yeah?" He turned her to face him and gave her a wicked grin. "Get out the cuffs."

"How original. Hey...knock it off," she said, squirming and laughing at the ticklish swipe of his tongue on the side of her neck.

"Just following orders, Deputy." He bit into the sensitive flesh below her ear, his arm tightening and bringing her flush against his body.

She went limp, letting him support her weight with his arm. How long had it been since she'd been held? Like this. By a man who wasn't her father awkwardly offering a shoulder to cry on. "Dinner smells good."

Ben chuckled, the low sexy rumble from his chest vibrating clear down to her toes. "I'm insulted."

"I haven't eaten since early this morning. Does that help?" Her eyes were closed. She only realized it when she had to force her lids up.

He'd lifted his head and was staring at her with a warm, sympathetic gaze. His smile was gentle. So was the hand stroking her hair.

Clearing her throat, she broke away. She didn't need sympathy. Not for doing her job. Not for any reason. She'd made her own choices. Some of them had been the lesser of two evils. But that didn't exempt her from owning them.

"Wow." A picnic was spread across the bed. Roasted chicken, ribs, potato salad, coleslaw, rolls and butter. "Did you wipe out the diner and the Food Mart?"

"I didn't know what you like." He grabbed the paper plates on the nightstand, next to the apple pie. "I almost asked Marge what you normally order. But that would've started rumors you don't need."

Touched by his thoughtfulness, she smiled at him. "Thank you."

"Yeah, well, there'll be enough speculation over what army I'm feeding. I scored real silverware, though." He held up a handful of knives and forks. "Of course, Marge made me swear a blood oath that I'd return everything."

"Ah, that's when she'll try to wheedle information out of you."

"I may need to borrow your gun."

Grace grinned. "I have a feeling you can handle Marge." Or any other female in his orbit, she thought, admiring his butt as he turned to clear a spot on the bed.

"It's tight in here. I should've asked if you'd rather eat in your room."

"This is fine." She noticed that he'd used towels to cover the bedspread before setting the food down. Even the single nightstand and small dresser were protected by paper sacks. The considerate gesture surprised her, though she couldn't say why. "How long did you live at the Sundance?"

The question clearly startled him. He gave her a funny look, then carried the only chair closer to the bed, the action slow and deliberate, as if the move required all his concentration. "Here, take this."

"I don't mind sitting on the bed. Or even the floor."

"Humor me."

Well, okay. Obviously he wanted to pretend he hadn't heard her. Though the question hadn't been a big deal until he'd sidestepped it so neatly. Still, she let the subject drop. "I'm sorry if this was a hassle, but I really didn't want to go out," she said, and took the plate he passed her.

"No hassle at all. It'll save time."

She eyed him warily, not sure if that was a smile lurking at the corners of his mouth. If he wasn't setting a trap, she'd be shocked. But she'd go ahead and play. "For?"

"Getting you naked."

"Huh. I was thinking the other way around."

"Just say the word, sweetheart."

"Sweetheart," she muttered and stabbed a chicken leg with her fork.

Ben. Completely naked. All that bronzed skin and hard muscle. Her imagination was barely up to the task.

A slight tremor shook her hand. Her heart beat harder and faster. Why now? It wasn't as if she'd forgotten for a single second where tonight would lead. Not since he'd followed her up the mountain. She'd known the moment she saw him standing behind her.

Okay, there might've been a lapse while she'd written

her report. Somehow she'd managed to block thoughts of him. Of them. Of tonight. But then she made up for it while showering the first time. The second time, too, come to think of it.

Scooping up some potato salad, she realized her appetite was gone. She was jittery inside, but in the best way. She considered telling him they didn't have to waste time eating. Although he had gone to a fair amount of trouble. They could always eat later.

She hesitated, her hand hovering over the rolls. Marge made them herself. Grace was totally addicted to them. She slid a glance at Ben.

He hadn't even started dishing up but was watching her. "Eat," he said, as if reading her mind. "You need to refuel, and we have plenty of time."

Just tonight, from what she'd gleaned. And that was good. Perfect, really. How much trouble could she get into in one night?

12

BEN LEFT THE door of his room ajar while he cleaned up and waited for Grace to store the few leftovers in her mini-fridge. They'd polished off most of the food. He'd never seen a woman put away as much food as Grace had. Many of the women he knew in Hollywood starved themselves. He smiled, thinking about Grace reminding him she hadn't eaten since breakfast, and then admitting she ate like that most of the time.

Hearing a knock, he turned to see her standing in the doorway, her gaze on the bed. He'd already stripped it down to the cream-colored sheets. They weren't bad for a small country inn.

"You didn't have to knock. Come in."

"I didn't want to startle you," Grace said, entering the room and closing the door behind her. "Must be hard for you to sleep on a queen-size bed."

"I'm used to making do. Can't be choosy when you're filming on location."

"Are you away a lot?"

"Pretty much. Lately, I've been working in Canada and Mexico. Cheaper for the studios to shoot there." He hoped he wouldn't be doing it much longer. Friggin' Lena. He squashed the thought and watched Grace glance around as though this was her first time in the room. "You nervous?"

"No," she said with a short laugh. "I'm really not."

"Good." He unclipped the cell phone from his belt, tossed it onto the nightstand and pulled her into his arms. "How would you like a rubdown?"

"Huh?"

Ben smiled at her wary, upturned face. "Don't look so suspicious. You're tense." He pressed his thumb gently into a knot in her shoulder.

"Ouch."

"See?" He brushed a light kiss across her lips, and damn, he was already getting hard. "Let's get your top off."

She yanked the shirt from her jeans. "I'll race you," she said, kicking her shoes to the side.

Caught off guard, it took him a few seconds to pull the T-shirt over his head. "What does the winner get?"

Grace was already down to a satiny blue bra. The color matched her eyes. Her skin was pale, a few freckles, but not too many. "Um, let's see…" She unzipped her jeans and slowly shimmied out of them, then bent forward, giving him just enough of a glimpse of her breasts to make him itch.

He caught her mischievous grin, and laughed. The little… She'd purposely distracted him. Fine with him. He liked her tiny panties. He'd like them better when they were on the floor. "Go ahead, finish stripping. You already won."

"I'll be sporting and let you catch up." She let out a muffled shriek when he locked her in his arms. A couple quick flicks and he unhooked her bra. "Hey!"

Damn, it felt good pressed chest-to-chest, but it would be better skin-to-skin. He shifted back, and the bra slid off her breasts. They were the perfect size, not too big, not too small, and they were real. With pretty, dark, pink tips that had already tightened into tempting buds. He rubbed his thumb over the left one and she gasped, her soft warm breath hitting his collarbone.

Just like that, his patience evaporated. He unzipped his fly and shoved the jeans off. The bra went flying toward the bathroom. He went for her panties at the same time she tried to pull down his boxers. She bumped her head on his chin and laughed, while he stayed focus on getting them completely naked.

The desperate need that made him clumsy and impatient shocked him. It wasn't about the need for sex. That he could find anywhere. He wanted Grace. Except this frenzied pace wasn't his style. He liked to take his time. Control the tempo, a slow, deliberate seduction that fed the fever.

"Ben?" Her face was flushed. "Let me do this."

He let her go and watched her crouch to slide down his boxers. Already rock-hard, his cock sprang free. Grace's eyes widened, shifting his heart rate from third gear to fourth. Warm, moist breath touched his hot flesh. With a harsh exhale, he caught her arms and pulled her upright.

She made a sharp sound, and his gut clenched. He didn't think he was squeezing too hard, but he released her. And noticed the scrapes and bruises from earlier. A Band-Aid covered the gash close to where his thumb had pressed into her arm.

"I'm sorry," he said, fisting his hands at his side. "I should've been more careful."

"It's nothing. You startled me, that's all." Her lips curved up. "I've had worse nicks shaving my legs."

"You're that tough, huh?"

"More than you know." Her smile turned bittersweet right before she stretched up to kiss him.

Their lips touched, and his hands automatically came up to caress her back, but he lowered them to his sides. He wanted to hold her, feel the softness of her skin, breathe in her heady womanly scent. But he'd do whatever it took to avoid hurting her. Just thinking about the possibility tempered his arousal. Something Grace had discovered for herself, judging by her sudden withdrawal.

"What's wrong?" she asked, blinking at him.

He shook his head. "Nothing," he murmured, looking into her uncertain blue eyes and then glancing at her scraped arm.

"Ben." She sighed, a quiet sound of weariness and resignation. "I know I'm not the kind of woman you're used to."

He smiled. "Okay, so I don't always date the sharpest tool in the box."

"I'm being serious. Sometimes my job is physical and I get banged up. It goes with the territory. I'm no hothouse flower. I can take a lot."

"I get it." And he did. Some of his stunt-women friends were the toughest people he knew. "That doesn't mean I can stop worrying that I'll hurt you."

She gave him a long, considering look. "Get over it," she said, shoving him so hard that he stumbled back and almost landed across the bed.

Quickly, he regained his balance and scooped her up. Her yelp was one of surprise, not pain, so he had no second thoughts about laying her on the sheets.

He sat at the edge of the bed and grabbed a pillow. "Lift your head."

"What are you doing?"

Ben waited for her to stop staring at his poor confused cock and do as he asked. A blush spread across her cheeks when she noticed he was watching her, and she let him slip the pillow under her head. "I'm gonna check you over."

"What?" Her voice broke on a laugh. "We're playing doctor?"

"Yep." He briefly kissed her mouth, noting a small scratch near her ear. Nothing to worry about. Brushing back her hair, he inspected her neck.

"You're being ridiculous."

He smiled. Very soon her doubts would be forgotten

as he touched all the places that weren't hurt. Using one finger, he traced a winding course down her arm, careful of the scrapes.

Grace shivered. Her "huh" made him look up.

"You're very good at multitasking." She smoothed the line between his brows. "Still, thank you for caring."

He stared at her for a moment, surprised that she could figure him out so quickly. But then he got distracted by her breasts.

Her nipples weren't as tight as before.

A couple strokes with his tongue took care of that.

She whimpered in protest when he stopped, so he lingered on each breast before trailing his lips between her ribs to her navel. He reached the spot just above the neatly trimmed triangle of hair, and she tensed. Squirmed. Tensed again.

Controlling a smile, he lifted his head. "Turn over."

"My back is fine. Not a single scrape."

"Glad to hear it. Turn over."

She came up on one elbow, her eyes narrowed. "Why?"

He brushed his fingers down the pale skin of her stomach. "Because you're beautiful, and I want to see every part of you."

A soft pink bloomed in her cheeks and spread to her ears. She flipped onto her stomach, probably to hide the blush. It didn't escape his attention that she was watching him from over her shoulder.

Much as he liked those pretty blue eyes, his gaze was drawn to her very nice ass. Stroking the swell of satiny skin with his palm, he asked, "Don't you trust me?"

"No."

"Not even a little?"

"Nope."

Ben smiled. "Good. Never trust anybody from Hollywood." He took a nip of her right butt cheek. "Especially me."

GRACE HAD NO time to think about what he'd just said. She arched her back at the amazing feel of his tongue tracing her spine with long, slow, feather-like strokes that overlapped and kept her off balance. How could she be so sensitive *there*? How did he even know?

He finally made it to the top of her back, then gently rearranged her hair so he had access to her neck. But instead of the kiss she expected on her nape, his warm breath teased the side of her breast. She nearly levitated at the misdirection. Playing fair, he cupped her other breast with a sure hand, fingers plucking lightly at her puckered nipple.

God, he was good at this whole drawn-out seduction thing. The way he made her moan and whimper gave her just enough rope, pushing her and pushing her, tempting her to beg because she feared he might stop. Making her want what he stubbornly refused to give.

Though really, it wasn't a surprise. Of course he'd be a master at handling a woman. What she hadn't expected was the tenderness. She wasn't even sure what to do with it.

Evidently, she'd have to figure it out another time.

On a low raspy groan, he slid his hand over her butt to the seam of her closed thighs.

They weren't closed for long. The combination of tongue and fingers was too much. She fisted the bottom sheet in her hands and didn't even try not to cry out.

Before she could draw her next breath, he put two fingers inside her.

Their moans were simultaneous.

He nipped at her shoulder. "God, you're so wet. So hot," he whispered, his voice an octave lower.

Then he started moving his fingers.

Her gasp was louder than she'd expected, but she was thrusting back as he showed her again that he knew what he was doing. The way he circled her clit with his thumb was enough to drive her crazy—slow as could be, forcing her to move, then fast, making her freeze, only to deny her at the edge of coming.

She couldn't decide whether she wanted to kill him or kiss him. Trembling like this was something new. Something that made her heart beat so wildly she could barely speak. Two heavy breaths later, he helped her turn over before he kissed her. Hard.

Grace kissed back, her hips lifting in search of his return. His hand, damp with the proof of her readiness, had trailed to her waist. By the time those fingers had made the return trip, Ben's tongue was already licking the same trail.

"You're killing me," she said, writhing as he teased her outer lips, never dipping inside where she so desperately wanted him. "Please," she mumbled, most of the word turning into a moan.

His hand moved to the top of her thigh. "You have no idea what you're doing to me," he said. "I can't think—"

"Then don't." She levered herself up, forcing his hand away. He was still on the edge of the bed, his cock heavy against his taut stomach. She rested on her elbows, meeting his darkened eyes as she spread her legs wider.

He moaned as if he'd been wounded and moved like a man on a mission. Two seconds later, his knees were between her thighs, pushing them apart while he leaned down to capture her mouth in a searing kiss. She could feel him trembling, as well. She would never have guessed he would be so affected. All those smooth moves had fallen away in a frenzy that made her tighten every muscle in her eager body.

"Condom," he whispered against her lips. Then he broke away to grab the packet off the nightstand. She couldn't help him get the thing open, not when her own fingers shook so hard.

Finally, he sat back on his haunches, sliding the condom down his cock, hissing the whole time. "So much for the massage," he murmured, more to himself than her.

Between them, there didn't seem to be enough oxygen in the room. Their panting only intensified as he slipped his hands under her thighs, lifting them and pushing them toward her chest.

Her body collapsed on the bed again, eyes wide, watching this gorgeous man prepare to enter her.

But first he lifted her right leg over his shoulder. She gripped him with her calf as he rubbed the head of his cock over her swollen center. She cried out, clutching the poor sheets once more.

He didn't make her wait any longer.

With one deep thrust, he filled her completely.

Grace bit her bottom lip to hold back a scream. Her body clamped down on him, making him groan and throw his head back. His harsh breathing stopped while he pulled back until just the head was inside her.

The next thrust was hard. He leaned forward, watching her face, building a powerful rhythm. The whole bed moved, forcing her to brace herself with a hand to the wall.

It felt incredible, especially when she was able to watch his abs tense and relax. Once she raised her gaze to his face, she wasn't about to look anywhere else.

Everything about him was focused on her. Every thrust, every gasp, every growl.

She'd never...ever... It was more intense than anything she'd done before. God, she was practically folded in half, but she didn't care. She wanted all of him. It was torture not to touch him, not to watch his slick cock moving in and out of her.

He leaned down until his lips were close enough for his breath to wash over her chin. Then he plunged his tongue inside her mouth in a bold, possessive move. Any other man, she'd have shoved away. Instead, she kissed him back just as possessively.

When he finally pulled back, he shook his head, whispered, "Grace," then closed his eyes. His body shifted until every thrust brushed her exactly where it counted. Over and over, the tension built until she couldn't hold back another second. Her orgasm swept through her entire body. It was like no other climax she'd had before, and for a moment it felt as if she seriously had levitated. Or maybe her mind had shut down.

A minute later, he stilled. He was in her as far as he could be, his back arched above her, the tendons in his neck stretched to the limit. Through tightly clenched teeth, he cried out, jerking as she squeezed, as she felt her own aftershocks.

He ended up next to her on the bed while she hogged the pillow. For a while, all they did was pant. A couple of times, they looked at each other, grinned, then went back to staring at the ceiling. Ben broke the spell.

"Now would be the time to roll over so we can go back to what we were doing before I was so rudely interrupted."

Laughing softly, she flopped a hand on his stomach, making him grunt. "If this is your end game, it really needs some work."

He rolled onto his side. Smiling, he brushed the side of her breast with his fingers. "I'm miles away from ending anything, and I hope like hell you don't think this was a game. I just wanted to work on those shoulders of yours while you're all relaxed."

"How can you even think of doing manual labor after—"

"Coming like there's no tomorrow? Having the best sex since I was fifteen?"

"What happened when you were fifteen?"

"My first time with a real girl."

"Okay, that's pretty exciting."

His grin made her laugh.

"I am going to turn over, but only so I can recover at my own pace." She was the one grunting when she finally got her limbs to cooperate. But she was pretty comfy when her head hit the pillow again.

He began to massage her upper back. After ten minutes of his hands kneading and coaxing knot after knot, she was officially wiped out. But she somehow managed to find her voice from the depths of her bliss. "I have to go back to my room soon."

"No you don't," he said.

"I really do." She moaned as he worked on a stubborn sore spot. "Also, if I don't have a chance to tell you later, this was fantastic for me, too. Maybe more than fantastic. Thank you."

His hand stopped. He kissed the top of her shoulder. "My pleasure," he whispered before he kissed her once more.

13

GRACE TRIED TO change positions, but something resting heavily around her waist stopped her. A memory from last night drifted into her foggy brain. Lazily opening her eyes, she smiled at the wall. Ben's arm tightened, drawing her closer until her butt was snuggled up to his...

"Jesus, Mary and Joseph." She shoved his arm away and bolted upright. Sunlight snuck past the drapes into the room. "What are you doing?"

She leaped out of bed, grabbing her jeans and searching for the clock. The box of condoms blocked it from view. They'd used three. She wondered how many were left.

Nope. Couldn't think about that right now.

Finding her panties would be good. "What time is it?" She found a sock. Not helpful. "The clock. Behind you," she said and got down on all fours to look under the bed. She spotted her bra on the floor across the room.

"Grace?"

"Please tell me it isn't seven-thirty yet," she said as she got to her feet. She'd worry about her panties later, she decided, and stepped into her jeans.

Ben was watching her, his lids still heavy with sleep. He pulled himself up into a sitting position, the sheets pooling at his waist, and her gaze was caught by the sight of his beautiful bronzed chest.

Part of her went a little gooey.

Nope.

She zipped and buttoned her jeans.

No way.

She couldn't let him distract her. "The time, please?"

"Come on." He smiled just as a lock of dark hair fell across his forehead. It made him look so damn adorable, she had to wonder if he'd orchestrated the whole thing. "It's not even six-fifteen. Come back to bed."

"I can't. I wasn't supposed to spend the night." She turned away before she threw good sense to the curb. "I have to work this morning."

"Think anyone would care if you went in late?"

"Yeah. Me."

"Yesterday was a tough day. You deserve to take the morning off. The guys aren't gonna say a damn word."

"Oh, do you get to take off from filming if you've had a bad day?" She found her top, then glanced at him. "Huh?"

Sighing, he scrubbed a hand over his face.

"I can't believe I spent the night," she muttered and scooped up the bra. Though she didn't need it just to go next door. "I swore I wouldn't do that." She pulled on her shirt. "God. This is ridiculous. I know better."

"Why?"

She'd purposely avoided looking at him, but now the edgy tone of his voice drew her attention. His steady gaze dared her to ignore him. She had no idea what was up with that.

"Why not spend the night?" he asked, perfectly calm, the challenge still in his eyes.

"I forgot my phone. No one could get in touch with me."

A slight frown creased his brow. Then he seemed to relax. "A small town like this? If anyone needed you, they would've come knocking."

"Yeah, exactly, and I wasn't in my room."

"Then they would've tried here."

"So not funny," she said and turned to the dresser to see if she'd left her key out. It wasn't in her pocket.

"Tell me something," he said, devoid of expression. "Is the problem with me, or would you feel this way about spending the night with any man?"

"I can't believe you have to ask." She stopped patting her pockets and met his eyes. "You know the guys have been giving me a hard time. And if you think the old double standard doesn't exist anymore, you're fooling yourself."

His unyielding expression cut right through her. She really thought Ben was more enlightened. When he held out a hand and gave her a surprisingly contrite smile, she realized the disappointment was aimed at himself.

"You're right," he said. "I shouldn't have taken it personally. I'm sorry."

Her conscience felt a small prick. She wasn't exactly guiltless. Her uncle's warning that Ben could hurt her chances at being elected sheriff had crossed her mind.

She moved toward him. "See? I should be keeping a whole football field away from you, and look what I'm doing."

"And what's that?"

"Walking smack-dab into temptation."

Grinning, he lifted the sheet and patted the mattress. "Slide in here for a minute."

"Yeah." At the sight of his arousal, she stopped and swallowed. She started to tell him to put the damn sheet down, but he'd like knowing he'd gotten to her. "A minute. Sure."

He shrugged, nodded. "Ten minutes. Sound reasonable?"

"Not going to—"

He moved quickly, capturing her arm as she tried to

back away. She let out a yelp, then laughed when he nearly toppled out of bed trying to hold on to her.

"I can't stay. I'm serious." God, he had no business looking this sexy so early in the morning. Dark stubble covered his jaw, making him look like an outlaw from an old Western Wanted poster. His hair was perfectly tousled. She didn't even want to think about what her mop was doing.

He ran his palm down her arm and brought her hand to his lips. Staring at her with those warm hazel eyes, he kissed the tips of two fingers and asked, "What time do you have to go in?" before moving on to the other three.

Emotion swelled in her throat. Last night, he'd been so gentle, so generous, so much more than she could ever have imagined. She hated that he'd be leaving for California soon. Maybe even today. The thought turned her stomach over. And yet she knew his leaving would save her. Save her from wanting too much and eventually getting her heart broken. Besides, last night had been possible only because she knew he wasn't staying.

Ben sucked the tip of her forefinger. "I know you have to work," he said, "so I'll try not to be a child." They both smiled. "After you've finished your shift, how about we go work out together? I'll show you a good place and give you tips to counter the altitude."

"Oh, thanks. That would be great." She really should've tried to sound more enthusiastic. How in the world could she be both thrilled and disappointed at the same time? He clearly wasn't leaving today. But he wanted to work out instead of…

His knowing smile made her blush. No, he couldn't actually read her mind. Although the man definitely had skills. Remembering one in particular made her cheeks burn hotter.

"Afterward, I'll wash your back. We'll get something to eat, and then…" He shrugged, a glint of amusement in his eyes. "I bet we think of something."

"I'm sure. But in the meantime…"

"I won't make you late," he said despite his tightening grip. Despite the fact he was pulling her closer. Close enough that she bumped into the bed. "One kiss before you go."

Grace drew in a deep breath. He smelled like sex. And trouble. The kind she couldn't afford. And she knew damn well what just one of his kisses could do to her. "One."

He nodded, his gaze lowering to her lips. "Then you're out of here. Even if you beg, I won't let you back in."

"Well, aren't you full of yourself?"

Ben didn't answer. Only smiled that lazy, arrogant smile of his. The one that bordered on lethal. She really should arrest him. Except he'd asked for her cuffs more than once last night. So, no, she wasn't about to play right into his hands.

He'd used the smile to distract her.

It struck her the second she felt his palm cup the back of her neck. Holding her captive as he nibbled and sucked at her lower lip. His tongue slipped inside her mouth, circling, teasing, tasting, and already she wanted more than just a kiss.

Before she realized what was happening, he'd slid his hand under her shirt to caress her unbound breast. Her palm had somehow landed on his cock. The sheet was an unwanted barrier, but she stroked him anyway through the soft cotton, feeling the heat from his skin.

He shuddered, then froze, before dragging his mouth away from hers and grabbing her wrist.

"Stop," he said, his voice hoarse and gruff. "Now, get out of here. Before I forget I gave you my word."

TWO HOURS LATER, Ben rolled out of bed. He picked up his phone and smiled when he saw Lena's number. She'd called just after midnight, then again at two, when she'd left a message. He put the terse voice mail on speaker while he stretched his arms and back. Lena sounded as if she'd had a few, and as expected, she was furious he'd involved her friends. By the end of her rant, she'd calmed down and was calling him "Baby."

Her behavior wasn't new, and man, he was tired of that bullshit. Tired of Hollywood and all the double-dealing, of the nods and winks that went on behind the scenes. Funny, he hadn't realized how much until he heard Lena's voice. Same old tango every time. Whoever had the most power led the dance.

After the night he'd spent with Grace, he wasn't so fired up to rush back to LA. He'd let Lena stew awhile before he called her. Although, she wouldn't be awake yet anyway.

Hell, *he* shouldn't be awake.

He glanced at the rumpled sheets, wondering if he'd be able to go back to sleep. He'd gotten so little of it last night. Grace hadn't fared any better. But she'd hit the floor revving up to eighty. Damn, he wished she didn't have to work. It would've been no use trying to coax her into calling in sick. Not when simply being unreachable had sent her into a tailspin.

And what had he done? He'd misread the situation and then overreacted. He should've known better than to take it personally. Grace would never consider him her dirty little secret. Apparently, everything wasn't about him. Go figure.

He'd been gone from Blackfoot Falls a long time. Whatever folks might've thought about him as a kid was old news. For some, now he was a hotshot Hollywood stunt man. And for others, he'd always be the McAllisters' maid's son.

Their problem, not his.

The thought surprised him.

As far as Grace went…last night, she'd showed him in many sexy ways what she thought of him. His body tightened with the memory of her scent, of the soft feel of her silken skin, how she gasped his name every time he entered her.

Giving his thoughts free rein would make for a long day. He glanced at the clock. Six more hours before he'd see her again. In the meantime, he needed to have a talk with his mother. Just before he'd picked up Grace on her run yesterday, Claudia had called. Their conversation had been brief. Mostly due to his sister's loss for words. Normally, she shot to Hilda's defense, no questions asked. Not yesterday. She'd been as confused as Ben over the exact month and year of their father's death.

After Ben showered, he grabbed coffee to go from the continental breakfast spread in the lobby and drove out to the Sundance. He didn't call ahead. Until he got things straight with Lena, he'd rather not discuss business with Cole. This time of day, Cole and most of the men were likely out in the pastures moving cattle or monitoring the new calves.

Ben parked his Porsche in the usual spot, relieved that he'd guessed right. No one was in sight. He skipped the front door and went around to the kitchen. Most likely that's where he'd find his mom.

He stopped at the bottom step to check under his boots. Hilda and Barbara McAllister's voices carried through the screen door, making him smile. Those two could talk about nothing for hours.

He was about to knock when he heard his name. Lowering his hand, he glanced around, then waited and listened.

"Why? It makes no sense." His mom's voice was muffled. A small mud room stood between him and the kitchen. But he recognized that stubborn tone of hers.

"I understand." Barbara sighed, sounding frustrated. "You know I do."

His mom's response was drowned out by the sharp clang of pots.

"Oh, for goodness' sake, Hilda. Ben's a grown man. Just tell him the truth. He can handle it."

Ben's gut clenched. Anger roiled inside him. Without waiting for his mom's response, he yanked open the creaky screen door. He entered the kitchen to find both women staring at him, their jaws slack, the surprise in their faces turning to dread.

"Yes, Hilda," he said in a cool, detached voice. He spared no pity as he met her frightened eyes. "How about telling me the truth for a change?"

GRACE ATE A hurried lunch while she drove back to town for a staff meeting. Like so many calls received by the Sheriff's office, the theft reported by the Circle K had turned out to be a false alarm. Apparently, people around Blackfoot Falls thought nothing of using the law to settle spats with their neighbors.

Talk about a waste of time when she could've been daydreaming about Ben instead.

The thought appalled her. She wasn't a foolish starry-eyed woman. Whatever was going on in her subconscious better snap out of it right now.

Noah had returned to town midmorning and called a meeting. It was probably nothing. He was leaving soon. And Noah was the type who wouldn't leave loose ends.

Just as she reached the town limits, it dawned on her. The reason for the meeting…maybe a decision had been reached on who'd be acting sheriff. Her hands got a bit clammy, and she wiped them on her jeans. No, Clarence would've said something to her. No way he'd be able to keep that to himself. Unless she was out of luck. Then he'd be too chicken to tell her in private.

Ten minutes early, she parked at the curb in front of the office. Noah's truck was already there. So was the other deputy's vehicle, as well as Wade's stupid hotrod. Something one might expect a kid to drive. Come to think of it, yeah, the car was appropriate.

She caught herself just as she opened the door and left the shitty attitude outside. All the guys were there, even Gus, the part-timer whom she'd met only once before.

Noah nodded and smiled. Slumped on a folding chair, Gus was busy shooting rubber bands at the file cabinet. Occupying the two desks the deputies shared, Wade and Danny greeted her with accusing glares. Roy refused to look at her.

So what had she done now?

"Since we're all here," Noah said, grabbing a bottle of water out of the ancient fridge, "we might as well get started."

Relief washed over Grace. No mayor, no announcement. Or so she assumed.

Noah perched on the corner of his desk. "Grace, take my chair," he said, his gaze briefly running down her scraped arm.

"I'm good right here. But thanks." She leaned against the opposite wall Roy had taken.

"I have several things I want to cover," Noah said, "but let's start with the incident yesterday."

Grace tensed, watching him pick up her carefully written report. No mention had been made of anyone but Ben. And simply because she couldn't ignore his possession of a department rifle.

"I see some out-of-town campers were given a scare." Noah looked up and scanned the room until his gaze rested on Grace. "This is an excellent report. Very thorough… but a couple things I don't understand. You asked a civilian for backup?"

Slowly exhaling, she stayed focused on Noah, who continued to look at her as if no one else was in the room. The tension was thick enough you could make soup out of it.

"Technically, I didn't ask a civilian—" she held in a sigh

"—ask Ben for assistance. I was at the Sundance getting information about the different trails since I don't know the area well enough yet and wanted to save time. Ben heard me talking to Cole McAllister, and later he followed me up into the foothills."

"You didn't think to ask another deputy for help?"

She opened her mouth, then shut it. Noah knew. He knew everything that happened despite the fact she hadn't snitched. Why he wanted her to spell it out, she had no clue. Whether he meant to punish the others or maybe call her to task, she didn't appreciate this public grilling.

"As I indicated in my report, since it was obvious the shooters were poachers, Roy advised me to call Fish and Wildlife." She swallowed a lump of pride and tried for a sheepish smile that went so acutely against the grain, she was glad for the wall's support. "Of course he was right, but I was stubborn, too eager to prove myself, I guess. I regret wasting time and county resources, and I have no excuse."

"In what way was it obvious?"

She hesitated. "I should've said, we *believed* the family wasn't targeted and the shooters were most likely poachers who didn't realize anyone was around."

Noah gave her a long, pensive look, then swept a gaze around the office. An eerie quiet descended. She sensed Roy and Danny fidgeting, but she resisted the urge to look at them.

Finally, Noah's eyes came back to her. "In your report, you mentioned Ben had possession of a department Remington. Did you give him the rifle?"

So far Grace hadn't lied, not really. Stretched the truth some, yes. And she was okay with that. But she could feel the heat climbing her throat as she paused to think about how she wanted to answer.

God, why hadn't he done this in private? From everything she'd heard, he was a good guy. "Ben followed me to help. I knew he could handle a weapon and I didn't want him defenseless." Her mouth was so dry she could barely swallow. "I see now it was another error in judgment that I also regret."

She tried to prolong eye contact with him. Tried and failed. A split second before she looked away, she saw a faint smile lurking at the corners of his mouth.

"You boys have anything to add?" he asked, then waited a good, very long, thirty seconds. "I didn't think so."

Grace stiffened and continued to avoid the others.

"For what it's worth, Deputy Hendrix, that wasn't the first time this department has accepted help from a civilian, and it sure won't be the last." Noah rose. "As far as going after the shooters, you were doing your job, and I commend you. Next time, give Fish and Wildlife a heads-up if you think you'll cross into government land. But that's it. You did everything right."

Roy noisily cleared his throat. "She asked me to go with her," he said, his voice low with shame. "Just before I came on duty. But I—I um—"

Grace stared at her feet. She didn't want this...

"No point in rehashing things," Noah said. "Grace's report is solid. I got some answers I needed. Who knows? Maybe a lesson was learned today."

Unfortunately for Grace, she looked up just before Noah's last words. Wade scowled at her. What an ass. She hadn't expected gratitude for sugarcoating the report, but she hadn't expected resentment, either.

Pumped with the sudden need to burn off some steam, she glanced at her watch. Two more hours until her shift ended. An hour at a firing range before she saw Ben would do the trick.

Danny didn't look as if he wanted to kill her in her sleep, so she asked him, "Where's the closest firing range?"

"Hell, sweetheart, don't you know how to shoot yet?" Wade kept his voice low enough so Noah couldn't hear, and gave her a sly smile. "You'll have to go to Kalispell for that. All us boys have been hunting and shooting from the time we started walking."

"Sometimes we target practice," Danny offered, and missed the dirty look Wade shot him. "Come with us next time."

"Thanks. I'd like that."

"How about today? After your shift?" Wade's sudden enthusiasm was pathetically obvious. So, he wanted to put her in her place, show the little lady how to shoot.

Grace smiled back. "Perfect."

14

IF THE THREE stooges didn't stop whooping it up over their exploits pretty damn soon, she was going to start shooting, and she wouldn't need a target.

Noah had agreed to cover the office so Grace and the other three could come out to Wade's brother-in-law's ranch at the same time. They'd all rode in Roy's truck, something she deeply regretted.

So far, she'd been completely excluded from every conversation, which, come to think of it, wasn't a bad thing. The call from Ben had been the best part of the ride, even though it had been cut short due to excessive nosiness.

One look at their final destination and Grace had to turn away from the stooges to roll her eyes. The "We're too good for a shooting range" gang had built a setup that rivaled the law enforcement range she'd frequented in Tucson.

The Triple D range, named by Wade, and to which she steadfastly refused to react, was part regulation, part jury-rigged, and all meant for overgrown boys. None of the deputies did a thing to help Wade's teenage nephews set up targets. At least protocol was being respected while they waited. All rifles were still packed away until the range was declared open.

Wade had called ahead, so the targets were almost ready. The three teenagers were hopping on one ATV and setting four targets at each distance. What she couldn't reconcile was a man like Wade building this good a facility. A fence with empty beer bottles? Sure. A 1000-yard course? Not a chance.

Right now, though, Grace just wished she had a reason to use her ear protection so she wouldn't have to listen to her coworkers.

"She was a live wire, that honey from the Sundance, wasn't she, Roy? Thought she might take off her top right there by the jukebox."

"Yeah, Wade," Roy said, his arms crossed over his chest. "She was a wild one."

Wade leaned toward Roy, but not until he'd glanced at Grace.

"She had plenty to show when we went back to my place." He used his hands to demonstrate the enormous size of the woman's assets. If she'd been that huge, Grace doubted she'd be able to walk without a cane.

"I swear," Wade continued, his voice rising even more. "I didn't know Arizona women were like that. Guess all that heat has to go somewhere."

Grace didn't roll her eyes. There had been so many aborted eye rolls since they'd started this trip, she was starting to worry about the health consequences.

The noise of the ATV racing toward the five-person firing line gave her the first relaxing moment she'd had since arriving at the ranch. Finally, they were going to get down to business. She headed for the farthest bay, but Wade stopped her. "This afternoon, we'll have to take turns. Too many rifles going off at once bothers my sister."

"And I'm guessing you'll tell us when we can shoot?"

"Danny'll go first, then Roy, then me."

"I'll be last."

"Yep," he said, struggling not to grin. It wouldn't have

mattered. His glee at her inevitable humiliation was written all over his face.

Grace simply smiled as she prepared her weapon. It didn't take Danny long to signal his round. There were targets at one hundred, four hundred, seven hundred and one thousand yards. The closer targets were round, the farther silhouettes.

She watched Danny shoot as she polished her scope. He wasn't terribly impressive, especially because he did all the shooting from a seated position, letting a tripod steady his weapon.

Roy was up next. He was decent up close, but she wouldn't want him to be point man at anything past four hundred yards.

But the show really didn't start until forty minutes in, when Wade got to the firing line.

Before he raised his Remington, she heard an automobile coming up the road. A quick glance told her it was Ben, although she'd recognize that Porsche's purr anywhere. He'd have to wait behind the flag until the shooting was over. But if he got out of his car, he'd see both the shooters and the targets.

Wade didn't look too happy about Ben showing up, let alone parking. "What the hell's he doing here?"

"He's my ride home. You going to shoot or what?"

After giving Ben one more scowl as he got out of his car, Wade walked to the line, put on his ear protection, then checked his chamber. He looked over his shoulder at Grace, and there it was again. The glare she'd come to know well.

He aimed and took his first shot. He was patient, which surprised her. And a decent shot, which didn't.

Of course, he used all four regulated positions instead of just plopping onto a chair. She imagined Roy and Danny didn't like to get dirty. But Wade had something to prove. He went from easy to hard: standing, kneeling, sitting, prone. Did a damn good job, too. He used the tripod only

when he sat, and all his hits were well within an accept-
able range with a few dead center. The way he grinned,
he looked like he expected a parade.

Now she was supposed to be so flustered by the big
boys with their big toys that she'd miss every target and
break down in tears. Jesus.

She put her gear together, taking some calming breaths.
Her ear protection blocking out the rest of the world, she
sighted the four hundred target and steadied her breathing. With a final exhale, she was in the zone.

Grace rode the circuit exactly like Wade had. By the
time she'd finished, she was flying on adrenaline. She
didn't need to see the targets the ATV boys were now
fetching. She'd aced it.

One look at Wade told her he had no problem seeing
where her shots had landed. She was never more grateful
to have a way out.

In a surprising act of defiance, Roy came into her bay.
"Good job," he said, his voice just above a whisper.

"Thanks. I can't believe the caliber of this range. I never
imagined—"

"It was Noah's plan, and Wade's brother-in-law did most
of the work. He makes some money off the deal."

"Huh." She finished stowing her gear, dusted off her
uniform shirt and jeans, then started toward Ben's car.
She didn't need to look back to know Wade was losing it.

She'd made it several yards when Wade said, "Ben
Carter. Figures. I heard she ran from Arizona because
her boyfriend dumped her. Left the whole department in
the lurch over some man. I'd bet my car she'll do the same
here because of that hotshot."

That stopped her. He'd said his vicious words just low
enough hoping Ben wouldn't hear. Stupid chickenshit.
Grace turned to face him. He should be just as afraid of
her as he was of Ben. "What?"

"Want me to say it louder?"

"Sure, go ahead. A lie is a lie no matter how loud you say it, or how soft you whisper. I didn't leave Arizona because of a man."

"That's not how Clarence tells it."

No. Her uncle wouldn't... "It's not true. Why would he say that?" Her voice had risen, but she stopped ripping into Wade when she saw the expression on his face. The anger over her cleaning his clock on the range was still there, along with a look of eager anticipation mixed with pure hatred.

She turned around before he could see fear get a crippling grip on her. *Stupid,* she thought, letting pride get in the way. After working so incredibly hard to leave her past behind, she'd just handed her fate to the most despicable man in Blackfoot Falls. No way Wade wouldn't start digging for dirt now.

BEN WAITED UNTIL she was settled in the passenger seat, then closed the door. Roy and Danny were staring, so instead of kissing her like Ben wanted to, he went around and slid behind the wheel. Jesus, how the hell had she learned to shoot like that? The woman could put a seasoned lawman to shame.

"I shouldn't have done that." Grace plowed her hands through her hair as they drove past the range gate. She yanked the elastic band from her ponytail and let the soft waves fall to her shoulders, the auburn highlights catching the sun. "So stupid. What the hell was I thinking?"

"Are you kidding?" He checked for any oncoming cars, then pulled onto the highway before glancing at her. She looked nervous, a little pale. "Did you see their faces? I thought Wade was going to pee his pants. I didn't even mind that bullshit he said about me."

"So, you heard him." She kept biting at her lip and shaking her head, small imperceptible movements that hinted at the battle going on inside her. "I know better," she said. "But I let Wade push my buttons, and I lost it."

"Hey, I'm surprised it took this long. The guy's an ass. He needed to be taught a lesson." Ben wondered again if he should've told her about the guys spiking her beer. "Maybe now they'll start showing you some respect." They came up on an old pickup loaded down with hay bales and passed it. "Obviously, you've had sniper training."

She winced. "You're speeding. Can you please not do that with me in the car?"

Ben slowed, but that's not why she'd reacted. He was going barely five miles over. She'd been uneasy before she got in the Porsche. Something was wrong. Something big enough to distract him from thinking about the bomb his mom had dropped earlier. "What's going on, Grace?"

She laid her head back and briefly closed her eyes. "Wade is probably wondering the same thing you are. And I don't need him or anyone else poking around in my past."

"I wasn't prying."

"No. Of course not. Anyway, I didn't mean you." She sighed. "Look, it's really nothing…" She trailed off, sighed again. "Actually, it's complicated. And personal, so not something I care to broadcast."

"Understood. Consider the matter dropped." Ben reached over and squeezed her cold hand. "To be honest, I was more interested in trying to sneak in a kiss without those mutts seeing us."

That got a small smile out of her. Then she turned to look out the window. "Clarence is unbelievable. Boy, wouldn't I love to catch him speeding. I'd write him a ticket so fast he'd go into a tailspin."

"Your uncle? The mayor?" Ben laughed. "You wouldn't do that."

"Damn straight I would." She shifted as if she couldn't get comfortable. "What Wade said about why I left Arizona? That's a lie. There was no boyfriend, no torrid affair.

Nothing even close." Her voice dropped off, her nervous gaze drifting back to Ben, but only for a moment. "I don't know what's wrong with Clarence. Making me sound like a hormonal teenager is likely to get me kicked off the ballot," she muttered.

So, she had her secrets. Everyone did. "Was this the first you heard of it?"

She nodded.

"I wouldn't worry about it. If version three of the story isn't circling the rumor mill by now, you're probably safe."

"I hadn't thought of that," she said with a laugh. "You do have a point. Anyway, I get the feeling people around here take Clarence with a grain of salt. Which makes him more of a liability in terms of my running for sheriff. So basically I moved here for nothing."

"Personally, I'm glad you did."

Her lips curved up a bit.

Okay, he got that it might've sounded like a bad line. But he meant it. If not for Grace, he would've been back in LA already. He hadn't spoken to Lena yet. She'd texted him that she was in meetings most of the day and would call later. Her tone had completely changed, so Ben wasn't worried. Still pissed, but not concerned that she'd squash the deal.

"What did you do today?" Grace asked. "Anything exciting?"

His throat went dry. The conversation with his mom hadn't completely sunk in yet. He'd tried talking to Claudia twice now, but his sister was just as confused as he, and they'd only gotten on each other's nerves by raising more questions.

"I was at the Sundance." He shrugged, unsettled by the impulse to tell Grace everything. It would be pointless. They didn't know each other that well. Or have much time left together. Talking about his messed-up life wasn't how he wanted to use it.

"Lucky you. It's beautiful out there." Grace started, then pulled out her phone. Probably had it on vibrate. She studied the screen, smiled and then slid the phone back into her pocket.

"You need to make a call? I can pull over and give you privacy."

"No, thanks. It's my dad. He usually texts me once a day. Nothing important." She shrugged, but sounded wistful. "Just to say hi and that he misses me. My mom died when I was young, so it's been just the two of us," she added as if apologizing.

"Nice that you have a close relationship with him. He's still living in Arizona?"

She nodded, the brief sadness in her face twisting his gut. Grace may not have run from a bad relationship, but something had chased her out of Arizona.

He thought of his mom, and what she had revealed to him this morning. How she'd fled Mexico, leaving behind her family and all she knew, running as far as the meager stash she'd hidden could take her and two young children. Her only goal had been to protect them. Hilda's strength and determination amazed him.

Ben glanced at Grace's profile, the delicate bone structure that hid the steel beneath, the scrapes on her pale arms. The two women were a lot alike, his mother and Grace. Both strong and courageous.

They drove in silence for a couple miles.

"Twelve years," he said, glancing at her. "The other day you asked how long I'd lived at the Sundance. I was six when we moved to Blackfoot Falls. Eighteen when I left."

He turned his attention back to the road. Already, he regretted his words and waited anxiously to see where the conversation led.

"Wow. It took you this long to do the math?"

Ben laughed. "Glad your mood improved."

She grinned, let her head fall back. Then abruptly

straightened as they approached the fork that would take them either to town or to the trails into the foothills.

He took the road leading away from town.

"Guess I should've reminded you sooner." She spread her hands. "Obviously, I don't have my running clothes. We'll have to swing by The Boarding House."

"You won't need them."

"What do you mean? I thought we were going to work out."

"We are."

"Ben?" Her eyes betrayed her excitement, even as she narrowed them in suspicion. "What are you up to?"

He smiled and steered them off the highway. The gravel road was bumpy and full of ruts. His poor Porsche. Damn, he wished he'd thought to borrow Trace's truck. Though Ben hadn't known in advance he'd take this detour.

Wide-eyed, Grace scanned the trees and overgrown shrubs. "Oh God, out here? Really?"

They caught a nasty dip.

He cringed and downshifted.

She bounced off the seat and grabbed the dashboard. "Should you be driving your Porsche on this terrain?"

"Nope."

"Ben. Stop. You wreck your car, and you'll never forgive yourself."

He finally applied the brake, pretty sure a dead branch had just done a number on the door.

"You're crazy," she said, staring at him in astonishment.

"You just figure that out?"

She leaned over the console and brushed her lips across his. "Crazy and trouble in one package," she murmured.

Before she could retreat, he cupped her face in his hands and kissed her. Her lips were soft and yielding, and damn, she tasted good. He'd waited all day for this. To be with Grace. He pulled back from the kiss, but he didn't go far.

He'd learned so much this morning, major stuff. World-shifting stuff. Everything he'd thought he knew was wrong. Or at least different from what he'd believed for so long. He wasn't okay with this new picture. Not yet. Maybe not ever.

The only thing he was sure of right now was that he wanted to be with Grace. If they had sex, that would be great, but it wasn't the reason he was so damn glad she was here with him. Through all the confusion, the jumble of strange emotions twisting him up inside, Grace had been at the back of his mind.

She slid her fingers through his hair, and he closed his eyes, enjoying her touch, inhaling the warm, clean scent of her skin. Letting the sound of her breathy sigh soothe the tension thrumming close to the surface.

She lowered her hand to his shoulder and broke the kiss. "What's wrong, Ben?"

He opened his eyes and saw the concern on her face. "You stopped kissing me."

"I'm serious. Something is...I don't know...different. Was there trouble at the Sundance?" She paused, blinked, and sank back against her door. "You're leaving for LA tonight."

"No." He shook his head. "Probably in two days, though."

Her nod seemed resigned.

"I could stretch it out another day if I let the Porsche rip. See if I can beat my time coming up here."

Grace hesitated. "No, you will not. The last thing you need is another ticket."

Ben chuckled. "Had to think about it, huh?"

Trying to hide a guilty smile, she lifted her chin. "I'm paid to uphold the law, not encourage people to break it."

"Right." In a minute he was going to strip those jeans off her. Then make love to her right here, in the open, on government land. He wondered what she'd have to say to that.

The humor left her face, and concern was back, clouding her beautiful blue eyes. "I promise not to bring this up again, but I want you to know I can listen if you need to get something off your chest."

It was tempting to make a joke or ignore the offer and get down to business. Time was short. She'd let him seduce her. But he was blown away that she could read him so well. And just maybe he'd subconsciously been putting out signals. Crazy as it was, he wanted to tell her. About his mom, his father...about everything.

Another minute snuck by as he weighed the pros and cons, but one more look at her anxious expression convinced him to go with his gut.

He reached over the console and gripped her hand. "I found out something today that knocked the wind out of me," he began slowly, realizing he didn't know where to start. Letting his guard down was scary as hell. Especially with a woman he actually cared about. He'd be handing Grace confirmation that he was a foolish, self-centered bastard.

"It's okay," she said quietly and turned her hand over so their palms met. "I'm not here to judge."

Jesus. The woman had a sixth sense. "It's family stuff. About how my mom, sister and I ended up in Blackfoot Falls." He glanced around. "Look, you want to get out of the car? We don't have to sit here."

"I'm good."

Not him. He was suddenly feeling claustrophobic. "I need some air."

"All right," she said, releasing his hand. "Let's take a walk."

He pushed open the door and heard a loud snap. Damn it, he'd forgotten about the dead branch. Wincing, he decided not to check for scratches. What good would it do? Whether he had to get the Porsche detailed or have it completely repainted didn't matter. What was done was done.

Too bad he couldn't paint over the shame of his past.

15

GRACE COULD TELL he was having second thoughts about opening up. What she didn't know was whether she should encourage him to talk or not. The last thing she wanted was to push him away. But if listening could help...

He came around the front of the car and took her hand. Choosing the wider of two trails, they walked side by side through the tall grass and purple wildflowers. The late afternoon air was starting to cool, and the dappled sunlight felt good on her skin.

After several minutes of silence, Ben said, "This morning, my mom told me something that was pretty hard to hear. About why she took us and left my father." Ben stopped, his sudden fascination with a stone he'd loosened with the point of his boot making her ache for him.

He looked like a little boy, all six-two of him. A little boy afraid to admit he'd done something wrong, and she wanted to wrap her arms around him, assure him it was okay.

Instead she said, "You're determined to wreck those boots, aren't you?"

His mouth curved in a faint smile, and he started walking again. "I have vague memories of my father. He'd be gone for weeks, but when he came home, he'd bring toys...

big things like a bike for me and a dollhouse for my sister. It always seemed like Christmas when Dad was around. For my sixth birthday, he surprised me with a pony. A month later we left."

Ben squinted up at a flock of squawking birds taking flight. "Antonio Campo. I just learned his name today. He was a businessman from Spain who'd just moved to Mexico when my mom met him. He was rich, good-looking, sophisticated, very European, and my mom..." Ben shrugged. "She was only eighteen and he was thirty. She'd just graduated from an all-girls' Catholic school, never had a boyfriend. When Antonio started sending her flowers and buying her jewelry, she fell hard.

"At first, her parents were on board. Here was this rich guy properly courting her, making large deposits in the bank where her father was president, buying up small businesses. Then the rumors started. That the money came from drugs, that he was laundering it through the businesses. About then, Antonio proposed, and my grandfather refused to give his blessing. He told my mom if she accepted, she'd be disowned."

Ben laughed unexpectedly.

Grace looked at him. "What?"

"I guess I'm more like my mother than I thought. She basically said 'screw you' and took off with Antonio."

Grace smiled. "Were they bluffing? Or did they really disown her?"

"Oh, yeah, they cut her off." Ben frowned. "It's weird to think I have grandparents. I'm not even sure how to refer to them."

"Has there been any contact? I mean, she did leave him."

Ben rubbed his eyes. "True, but the rumors were only the tip of the iceberg. Antonio wasn't someone you messed with..." He paused, his jaw clenched so tightly that the muscles in his neck flexed. "He bought a huge white house with extensive grounds and gardens. Then he put up a ten-foot iron fence around the whole thing. I don't remember much. I saw some pictures today. The place was really something, more like a compound with living quarters for the help. Which included armed guards.

"My mom's dream house ended up being her prison. Turned out Antonio was the right-hand man to the head of a large and very brutal cartel. The day his boss disappeared, Antonio took over."

Ben slowed to a stop, his gaze avoiding hers. Grace connected the dots, and she ached for Hilda and the decisions she'd faced.

"Mom knew he could be violent and cruel, though he'd always treated us well. But it was clear that if she tried to leave or ever crossed him…" Ben looked at her. "No one would find her body."

Grace nodded, knowing too well what he'd said was true. Her work on the task force dispelled any illusions. "What made her finally take the risk?"

"She overheard Antonio telling me that soon I'd be joining him in the *family business*. That was her breaking point. She knew if she didn't get Claudia and me out of there, our lives were over anyway. My mom—" The catch in his voice brought a lump to Grace's throat. "She didn't contact her parents. Antonio liked that she was estranged from them. So she hoped that if they weren't involved, he'd leave them alone. She was too afraid and ashamed to risk a card or phone call."

He turned away again and let his head fall back. "After all she's been through, after all I've put her through, she's never let go of that shame." Ben sighed, the sound both sad and frustrated. "I can't imagine the courage it took for her to leave him."

Grace wanted to touch him, but she held back. It wasn't time for comfort yet. "How did you end up in Montana?"

"We rode buses and stayed in cheap motels until the

money ran out. And then she met Barbara McAllister. I still don't understand why she gave my mom a job. She had no skills, couldn't even cook. Her parents had money and servants, the whole thing, so she'd grown up without having to lift a finger." He laughed without humor. "It's so damn ironic, her ending up a maid, housekeeper…it doesn't matter. To think I hated when people referred to me as the McAllisters' maid's son."

His reaction to her not giving Trace a ticket made sense now. "So your grandparents never really knew what happened to all of you?"

"No. Well, early on, Barbara McAllister asked an aunt to mail a letter from Kansas saying we were all right and headed to Canada. Just in case Antonio managed to intercept it. Mom prayed her parents knew enough at that point to stay away from Antonio. Since then, she's gotten word to them twice, with both letters postmarked in Canada. Five years ago, she learned Antonio had been killed. But she'd already told Claudia and me that he'd died four years earlier. Another lie. But I understand now. I was twenty-four and still wanting to search him out, and she hoped that would make me back off. Unfortunately, by the time he actually was killed, her mother had been diagnosed with Alzheimer's."

"Oh, Ben. I'm so sorry," Grace said, though words seemed inadequate.

"Yeah, me too." He sighed. "My mother had it tough, and I didn't make it any easier for her. When Claudia and I started asking questions, of course Mom had to lie. First she told us we were from Texas. Then it changed to Florida. As I got older, I noticed the inconsistencies and called her on every one of them. I was a real prick."

"You can't blame yourself for wanting answers. What child doesn't?"

"I'm talking about later, when I was in my teens."

"There's a good reason teenagers can't legally drink

or vote," she said in a teasing tone, but she could see he'd already condemned himself.

"After high school, I threatened to go look for him. Then suddenly she'd *heard* he'd left the country. I knew it was another lie. A month later, I took a roan from the stable to ride up to Big John Flats. I didn't tell anyone. I'd done it before, and I was gone for only thirty minutes. But when I got back, she came running out of the house yelling that I wasn't a McAllister and had to stop taking things without permission."

He kicked the ground again, hard. "I saw red. I was embarrassed and sick to death of being reminded I was the help." He held his breath for a long moment before he let it all out. "The McAllisters never treated me that way. In fact, Gavin and Barbara sat me down that same night and told me nothing had changed. I was family, no different from their own boys. I should forgive my mom because she'd been frightened that I'd run off. I thanked them, packed what could fit in a duffel bag and left the next morning. That was fifteen years ago."

Grace blinked. "This is the first time you've seen your mother since you left?"

He nodded.

"Oh. Wow."

"Yeah," he said. "For months, no one knew if I was dead or alive. I finally called my sister. Wouldn't even tell her I was in LA. I wish my mom had just told me the truth. I was eighteen…I could've handled it."

Grace started to say something, reconsidered and pressed her lips together.

"What?" Ben studied her. "Say it."

She stared back at him, knowing this was a no-win situation. "She was right not to tell you." Grace saw the defensiveness in his eyes. "Clearly, you were too angry to think rationally."

"I was mad because of the lies. It was obvious she was

hiding something." He exhaled, the sound harsh with frustration. "Sure, I was curious about him, but I wasn't gonna look him up and bond over his drug business. Don't get me wrong...I'll always regret putting her through hell. But a lot of time passed between her lie that he was dead and his actual death. I was an adult, and should've been given the choice. Now my options are gone."

Given the way he'd left home, Grace doubted he'd been emotionally ready for the truth. Even now, he was having trouble processing the new information. He'd been living on uncertainty and suppositions, and now the world as he'd known it was crumbling. A world where he'd been the victim, the person wronged. Now he had to come to grips with an entirely different scenario.

It would take a lot of time for their family to heal. God, she ached for all of them.

Ben stared up at the sky and Grace let him be. Several yards ahead, the trail veered to the right of a small clearing. She heard water and followed the sound to a stream, bubbling over and around rocks and branches. Crouching, she scooped a handful of the cool water and splashed her face.

"Sorry for unloading."

She smiled up at him. "It's fine. I just wanted to give you some space."

"I figured you'd written me off."

"Stop it."

"If you knew what a complete bastard I've been—"

"Shut up. Or I'll—" She couldn't find the right words.

His lips twitched. "You'll what?"

"I'll arrest you."

Giving in to the smile, he helped her to her feet. "For what?"

"Noise pollution. You're hurting my ears with a bunch of crap."

"Ah." He put his arms around her. "Let's see if I can

make it up to you," he said, and kissed the spot behind her earlobe.

"You're on the right trail."

BEN HUFFED A laugh and tightened his hold. "That was actually pretty funny," he said, his breath heating her damp skin.

Her hand moved up his back. "I'm occasionally witty."

"Sexy, too."

She sighed as he rocked her body. "With the right motivation."

He pulled back just far enough to look at her, to make sure she meant what he thought she meant. "Challenge accepted," he said.

"Right out here? In the middle of the woods?"

It wasn't as if he didn't know what she was doing. He'd just revealed more about his life to her than to anyone he'd ever met. She didn't seem shocked or appalled, at least not at him. He hadn't realized how much he needed her teasing smile and her welcoming body until he'd pulled her close. "Right out here," he said. "I'd never make it to town. But this is perfect. No one will hear when I make you scream."

She was the one to pull him into a kiss. And not just any kiss. Both of her hands cupped his face, and her tongue gave his a wicked workout. Not quite what he'd promised her this morning, but so much better.

While Grace had them both busy from the neck up, he started working on her buttons. She bowed her back as soon as she realized his objective, and he finished the job in record time.

"Don't forget you," she said, giving them both a chance to catch their breaths.

"Kiss more," he said, unhooking her bra with one flick. "Talk less."

She laughed. Then she kissed him again and moved her thigh between his legs, rubbing him right where it counted.

He couldn't hold back a moan, and now the race was on. To get them both naked, to remember the condom in his pocket before maneuvering them down to the grassy clearing, and damn, whatever was next was wiped clean away as both of her hands moved from his face to his other cheeks.

She gave him a nice squeeze just as he thought he'd be able to push down her jeans and panties in one quick swipe.

"You okay, stunt man?"

"That sassy mouth of yours is going to get you into trouble one day."

"I think I can take care of myself."

"Hell, woman. I saw what you can do with a rifle. I didn't say you'd get in trouble with me."

She grinned. "You want me to let go?"

"Only because there are bigger and better things to come."

Grace laughed. "Ah, so modest."

"Yep. How about you take off your shoes while I get out my wallet?"

She quirked an eyebrow. "Excuse me?"

"Condom."

"Right. Okay, shoes."

He hated letting anything get between them, even the cool afternoon breeze, but there was nothing to be done except get his boots off while he got the condom out. By then, she was barefoot and topless. He could almost feel his tongue swirling around those beaded nipples as she bent over his eager—

"More stripping, less drooling."

He hopped to it. Literally, but he finally was barefoot, as well, and he wasted no time stripping down to the skin.

Once they were naked, he did a slipshod job of setting out his jeans and shirt on the ground as a blanket. It didn't matter. He would have lain down if the grass were on fire.

"Wait, what are you—?"

God, she looked gorgeous with her hands on her bare

hips, her breasts rising with each breath. He waved her closer as he lay back. "Straddle me."

THE COOL AIR wasn't quite enough to keep up with the heat between them.

Grace gasped as she rose a little higher. The trick was to keep him inside her, but only just.

"You're going to kill me," Ben said. "Dead."

"It's okay," she said, her voice as wobbly as her thighs. "I know where you keep your car keys."

Her knees on the thick, cool grass, she gripped Ben's hip bones like handles. He'd lowered his butt to the ground, but she hadn't gone with him this time. Instead, just before he slipped out of her, she tightened her muscles around the crown. She wouldn't be able to hold him for long like this, but she sure did like how it felt.

What she hadn't counted on was his next thrust. He was so strong, he pushed through until he was all the way inside her. After going at it hot and heavy for at least half an hour, this lift was as high as the first.

Once she regained the ability to speak she said, "How are you able to do that? I'm not exactly light as a feather."

"Sheer will."

As cocky as he was, she knew he couldn't keep up this pace forever. She was thinking very hard about moving a lot faster herself, but the way he seemed to be drinking her in made her clench.

The problem was, he hadn't touched where she needed to be touched.

It was time for her to take it to the next level. First, she closed her eyes. She couldn't think when she was looking at him, at the five-o'clock shadow that made him look mysterious, or the way he'd lick his lips as if he wanted to eat her right up.

Ben touched her cheek. "Look at me."

His voice was velvet and grit, and she automatically

obliged. Again, he thrust to the hilt, the connection between them electric, a sizzle that reached every part of her. She squeezed her muscles around him, and oh, she could see he was getting close. It was his turn to fight shutting his eyes as she lowered herself once more.

"What the hell are you doing to me, Grace?"

"I'll stop if you want me to—"

"God, no. Don't. Please."

She doubted he saw her smile. "I'm close, Ben. All you need to do is touch me."

"Already?"

"Knock it off or I really will stop. Come on. I need both hands to balance."

"If you kiss me," he said, finally looking up at her, "we'll be at just the right angle. No hands needed."

She grinned. He was brilliant. She leaned forward until their lips were inches from each other. He almost closed his eyes again, so she bit his chin, just enough to get his attention. "Hey, kiss more," she whispered seconds before she made her move.

The kiss was meant to be hard and sexy and full of sass, but it quickly softened from all the tenderness that had been building since he'd offered her his vulnerability and trust.

He stilled, lowering himself to the ground. He cupped the side of her face as he pulled back from her mouth only to kiss her chin, the tip of her nose, then a soft kiss on her parted lips.

"Grace." His hoarse whisper made her shiver.

As she kissed him again, his hip arched slowly. She gasped when she felt the base of his cock rub just right. Their faces were very close, but she knew he was smiling the whole time. She blinked in delighted surprise. She'd expected a little rub, but what she got was so much more. The next time she kissed him, he did it again. And again.

She moved a bit to the left, and he set a bruising pace.

Her muscles tightened, and she couldn't concentrate on anything but the oncoming storm. Gasping and trembling, she knew it wouldn't be long…

She came like a powerhouse, loud enough to chase the birds from the trees. It was messy and wonderful. He just kept going until he cried out and came with a tremendous shudder, and they both collapsed like gasping rag dolls.

It took Grace a while to figure out they weren't moving. Not below the chest, at least. After the best workout ever, all they were both good for was filling their lungs.

Without any warning, she rolled off him, onto the grass. "Oh, for God's sake."

"What's wrong?"

She tried to lift her head but gave up instantly. "We're going to have to sleep here because I'll never get up again."

"I'll help you," he said with great assurance.

She managed to turn her head to face him, just as he turned his. "Who's going to help you?"

He grinned. "I think there are some edible berries somewhere near here. If not, there's always bugs."

She sat up with a great heave. "Unless there's a Starbucks behind that tree, we're going back."

16

BEN HELD THE door open for Grace, and she gave him the eye roll he expected before getting into the Porsche. "What, I'm not supposed to be polite because we're in the woods?"

The minute he got behind the wheel, she was ready with a retort. "I figure sweaty sex and cleaning up in a stream—without towels—meant neither of us had to be polite for about a week."

"Hey, I dried you with the shirt off my back."

"I appreciate that. My breasts have never been drier."

Ben laughed. "And don't forget, I remembered the condom."

"Fair enough," she said as she settled into her bucket seat.

He took the drive to the highway slowly, reminding himself that the scratch on his door was worth it. Which it was. Cars could be fixed, even beauties like this one.

When they were safely on the highway headed for town, he finally looked at Grace. The worry etched in her face was definitely not expected. "What's wrong?"

"Nothing."

"Grace."

"It's nothing for you to worry about, just that business with Wade. I was an idiot to pull that stunt today. I know he's a jerk, and I could have avoided all of this by not showing off."

"Seriously? Wade? He's a moron. Besides, what could he possibly find out about you?"

"Plenty," she said, then hesitated. She was staring straight ahead. Her jaw was tight, and so were her shoulders. Another glance and he saw that her thumb was rubbing her finger rough and fast, all of which made him realize this thing with Wade was far more than it appeared. Grace was giving too many signals for him to back away now. Instead of making a joke, he waited, concentrated on driving, snatching glances at her when he could.

When he'd pretty much given up on her talking to him, she said, "Back in Arizona, me and my partner from the task force—we were eating dinner in our vehicle. Honestly, we were arguing more than eating. Out of nowhere, some guy barrels out of the corner market holding a .357 Magnum. The bastard shot into the store before the door closed behind him. T.J. jumped out of the car. A minute later, he was…"

She took a couple of breaths and lowered her gaze to the console. Ben wanted to pull over, but he was scared Grace would stop talking.

"He'd been acting weird for a while. Asking me to cover for him at work, which, okay, we have to sometimes, but then he was asking me to cover for him with his wife. He knew she and I were friends. But T.J. was my partner. That trumps everything. I don't know if you can understand—"

"I do incredibly dangerous stunts for a living. I know what it is to trust."

She nodded, and he focused once more on the mostly empty road.

"Him keeping me in the dark was unacceptable. I had his back, but people were jumping to wrong conclusions— that we were having an affair—and the last thing I wanted was for the task force to lose faith in us, and God forbid, for his wife to hear the wrong thing."

Grace sighed, and he put his upturned hand on her thigh. Lightly. Expecting nothing. But when she immediately entwined her fingers with his and gripped him tight, something deep clicked into place.

"He told me he'd been having an affair with the captain's wife. That was bad enough, but then he told me the captain was abusing her. So of course, T.J. was trying to get her away from him on the QT. The captain had a lot of clout. T.J. couldn't report it. I hate to say it, but he was right not to."

"Yeah, there's a lot of loyalty when you're in a job that can cost you your life. It sucks when it's used to protect the wrong people."

She didn't deny it. "I told him to go to Internal Affairs. That I'd help him get the wife and her two kids away without anyone being the wiser. But he had to stop sleeping with her. For everyone's sake."

Grace squeezed his hand again as she looked at him. "I understand how dangerous it was for your mom to escape Antonio. The task force I was part of? It was to take down Arizona's largest dealer. We'd been at it two years, and we were close to the crafty bastard. Damn close. T.J. needed to get his head back in the game, and he wasn't going to do that if he was working solo to help Marie."

"Well, shit. That's a hell of a spot to be in. For him and you."

"For everyone on the task force." With her free hand, Grace picked up the water bottle he'd left in the cup holder for her. She offered it to him, but he shook his head.

"T.J. wasn't supposed to go after the gunman, not like that. It was a rookie mistake. By the time I yelled his name, he was already dead. Bullet through his head. I didn't even catch the guy. A uniform cop did. Someone I didn't know."

Ben pulled onto the turnout five miles outside of town.

"What are you doing?"

"Stopping for a minute." It was getting dusky and her face was in shadows, which was for the best. "Go on."

"There was an investigation. The rumors about the two of us were starting to spread. It was just a matter of time before T.J.'s wife heard. I couldn't do that to her. Or their kids. So when the brass inferred I might not have provided adequate backup, I let it go.

"I was cleared by IA, but I'd already been condemned. I told Glen—he was the investigator—everything. I couldn't help the captain's family on my own. Even knowing I could trust IA completely, I was tainted in the eyes of the Tucson police, the sheriff's division, pretty much everyone. No one would want to partner with me, not on the task force or my department."

Ben wondered if she knew that while her voice was completely stoic, there was no hiding the hurt in her face. She looked defeated. And that got to him in a way he hadn't imagined possible.

"The best thing to do was for me to leave. To let everyone think I might've been partly responsible for T.J. getting killed. That way, T.J.'s family could keep their memories of a loving husband and father and receive compensation. The captain's wife would be moved somewhere safe. Eventually. After the task force makes their bust. I hate that part, but…you know, the greater good and all…" She shrugged.

"Internal Affairs agreed to that plan?" Ben asked.

Grace straightened, and he watched the warrior come back. "The task force was at risk. It was in all our best interests for me to disappear so everyone could get back to focusing on what was important."

"It sure as hell wasn't in your best interest. There's no way you made the decision to leave. If that guy from Internal Affairs had any sense at all, he'd have done everything in his power to talk you out of it."

Grace sighed. "He did try." She looked Ben in the eye.

"There's only one other person who knows what happened. That's my father, who's a retired sheriff and also happens to be old friends with Glen. Dad hated to hear that I'd be taking the blame, but he understood. So, yes. I made the decision, and I have no regrets. And now you know."

He wanted to swear that he wouldn't say a word, but she wouldn't have told him if she didn't already trust him. "So how is a little worm like Wade gonna find out anything about this?"

"If he makes a phone call to the right big mouth, it's possible he'll hear everything. Or the version that makes me look like a piece of crap."

"Well then, leave. Damn it, Grace, you're too good a cop to be wasted in this hick town."

"It's fine," she said, releasing his hand only to push her fingers through her hair. "As long as T.J.'s wife never finds out about the affair, screw Wade, I don't care what that idiot learns. She and the kids have been through enough. They all worshiped him."

He knew better than to argue. What Grace really needed right now was support and trust. He'd do whatever it took to give that to her.

Instead of kissing her until morning, which he very much wanted to do, he said, "Hey, why don't you come with me to the Sundance tonight? I can promise you my... the McAllisters will make you feel comfortable."

He had almost called the McAllisters his family when only his mom fit the bill. What the hell? But the truth was, the Sundance really was his home, and he was as close to the McAllister brothers and Rachel as he was to Claudia.

Odd that he'd never once felt like LA was anything more than a means to an end. Certainly not his home.

"I can't," she said. "I've got things to do. I need to call my old boss. Do some damage control. And you need to spend some time with your mom. You're going to be leaving soon, and you're just getting to know her."

The truth of that stopped him. "Isn't there anything I can do?"

"You've already done so much. It felt good to say it out loud. I doubt I'll ever tell anyone again. So, no, there's nothing more you can do. Just know that I appreciate it. All of it."

He smiled. "So maybe we can hook up when I get back from the Sundance?"

Grace settled in her seat. "Maybe. If I'm not asleep." Though he couldn't pinpoint it, something in her tone bothered him. He sure hoped it wasn't regret.

LENA HAD LEFT two voice mails before Ben could get back to her. Fresh out of the shower, he hit speed dial. She answered on the second ring. "Where are you?"

"Hello, Lena," he said, keeping his voice neutral, his temper in check. "You want to tell me what's going on with the loan?"

"You call my friends? What the hell were you thinking?"

"About the loan." He put her on speaker and pulled on his jeans. "You backed out. Why?"

"I had no idea if you were still interested. You take off half-cocked for Montana in the middle of everything. What was I supposed to think?"

"Jesus." Yeah, just what he figured. She was being pissy because he'd left. "I told you two weeks ago I had this wedding."

"And I distinctly remember telling you we had a conflict. The awards dinner?"

"Come on, Lena, you can do better than that."

She hesitated, but he could picture those red-tipped claws coming out while she weighed her options. "So, are you in or not?"

"I'm in. I've always been in." He pulled a blue shirt out of the narrow closet. "Are you?"

"You're sounding rather cocky. You have a sudden windfall I don't know about?"

Ben gritted his teeth. Jesus, how often had Lena pulled this crap? She always needed to be in control. The only reason he was in this with her at all was because he knew once he was running the ranch full-time, she'd back off and leave him to manage things. "I'll be here another few days, then head back on Saturday morning."

"Why not leave today? The loan papers are waiting for our signatures."

"We've been approved?"

"Of course."

Relief poured into him, blunting his annoyance. He thought about Grace. He wasn't about to jump through more hoops for Lena, not when Grace was so sure the shit was about to hit the fan. No way he'd leave her to face it alone. "Saturday is the soonest I can get out of here. I had some trouble with the Porsche. It should be ready by then." He'd done a number on the paint job, so it wasn't an outright lie.

"You're letting some hick mechanic work on it?"

"I'll call you once I'm on the road."

"Fine. The minute you leave…"

Ben shook his head. "I have to go," he said, and disconnected before she started pouting.

He wanted those papers signed. Owning half the ranch would change so much for him. He'd had the urge to return to ranching for a long time. But it had never been stronger than now…since he'd come back to Blackfoot Falls.

He buttoned his shirt, staring at his phone and wondering if he could change Grace's mind about going with him to the Sundance. She was suffering because of her moral choice to take the high road. Something he hadn't seen since…well, since learning the truth about his mother. He'd gotten so used to the backstabbing Hollywood bullshit that he'd forgotten there were good people in the world. Strong people. Like Grace. Sitting in her room stewing wouldn't do any good. The more he thought about Wade's face after Grace spanked the hell out of him earlier, the more inclined Ben was to consider she might have reason to worry. The guy was just plain stupid. And that made him unpredictable. If he had half a brain, he'd realize he was outsmarted and outclassed and should keep his damn mouth shut.

Grace had mentioned she might contact her old boss, find out if the talk had died down. Maybe warn him that Wade might call and stir things up. That could be a good idea, or it could backfire. He was a little surprised how much it mattered to him that her honor in doing the right thing could come back to bite her in the ass.

Even so, Grace wouldn't give in and take the easier route. The longer he knew the woman, the more he admired her.

As he got his wallet and keys off the dresser, it dawned on him again that the loan had gone through. Tonight, maybe he'd talk to Cole about the stock. Although it might be smarter to wait until the papers were signed.

Once he was in the hallway, locking his door, his thoughts circled back to Grace. It could get sticky if Lena decided to delay things. He hoped not, but he wasn't about to leave just because Lena was playing head games. Not even for the Ventura ranch.

He stopped cold.

For the past six months, every career decision he'd made, every dream he'd dreamed had led to owning a ranch and working with horses again. Stunt work paid damn well. His agent had thought he was crazy, and who knew, maybe Ben was a little loco from too many concussions. But damn it, he liked Grace. A lot. And he supposed he had stronger feelings for her than he'd had for a woman in a long time. Okay, if ever...

But...

Ah, hell, he didn't know what to make of her. Or the

way he felt. He'd never had an easier time talking to anyone. When he was with Grace, he didn't want to be anywhere else. The sex was awesome, too, so yeah, of course he had *feelings*. He wanted to crawl into bed with her right now. And he would, later, after he got back from the Sundance.

GRACE LOOKED UP from her book and glanced at the alarm clock again. It was five minutes past eleven, and five minutes since the last time she'd checked. She certainly knew it was true that no good deed went unpunished. It wasn't enough that she'd had to leave her job and her old life behind forever. Now she might be falling for a man who'd be gone in two days.

Not to mention that her career could once again be in jeopardy.

It was her own fault. She'd been careless and arrogant, pushing Wade too far and then ignoring the possible repercussions. Even knowing Wade would make trouble, she'd gone off with Ben instead of focusing on cleaning up her own mess. She could've asked him to bring her straight home. If she had, she might've made the call to her former boss in time to prevent Wade from digging up the rumors that had sent her packing.

The stupid jerk had worked fast.

No, that was just an excuse. She'd screwed up twice.

Regardless of the whole Wade fiasco, she'd known spending time with Ben was dangerous, that when she was with him, she couldn't control herself.

It wasn't like her to get so into a man she barely knew. She'd never entered relationships quickly or easily. The last time she'd gotten semiserious was in college. She and Eric had stayed together at the University of Arizona for two years. Then he'd taken a job in Pittsburgh, and they'd ended the relationship with very little drama. Of course, she'd been sad. Breakups were hard, but she'd gotten over him.

Then again, she'd never felt *this* with Eric.

She tossed her book aside. No use trying to read. All she could think about was the mess she'd made. And for what? Ben was leaving.

He'd probably come back a couple of times a year to visit his mother. She groaned. She'd be gutted the first time he came home with a woman.

Damn. Ben wasn't supposed to have been here long enough for this to happen. She certainly hadn't meant to trust him with her secrets. And her heart. But she had, and now she had to figure out how to stop thinking about the man who could have been... Nope. Not going there.

She adjusted the pillows behind her back. Tomorrow was going to be a bitch. And yet, here she was dressed and ready to see Ben, furious at herself for even considering seeing him again tonight. Hadn't she screwed up enough for one day? For a lifetime?

God, she wasn't a stupid person. How could she have so blithely underestimated Wade? He'd already gotten to someone in her old office.

The soft knock on her door had her holding her breath.

It took all of her willpower not to let him in. Then she remembered he'd be gone in no time at all, and the pull came back. But the only person she could count on here in Montana was herself. When she was with Ben, the rest of the world disappeared, and she couldn't afford to let her guard down again. She needed to cut this off right now before she did something else stupid. No one knew better than her that impulsive decisions had consequences. So even as he called her name, she kept her mouth shut, put her book under the covers and blinked away the tears.

17

THE STARES AND whispers started shortly after lunchtime the next day. Grace drove back to town and parked the truck between the office and The Watering Hole. Then headed to the bar to respond to a robbery call from Sadie. Before Grace had hit the sidewalk she noticed several curious looks and could feel the buzz in the air.

Amazing how small-town rumors could spread as quickly as wildfire. At least she hadn't been caught off guard. Though she wasn't sure if that made things any better since her tummy had tightened into a giant knot. She tugged at her blue ball cap, wondering if she should bother replacing it with a Stetson to go with her uniform shirt. She might be fired today. Wouldn't take long to find out.

She smiled at a pair of elderly white-haired ladies who could be twins. They stood at the curb as if waiting to cross the street, though no cars were coming. One of them smiled back. The other woman's eyes widened, and her cheeks turned a bit rosier.

The Watering Hole wasn't open for business yet, but Sadie said she'd leave the door unlocked. Something she did often during the day. It was no wonder cash was missing from the register. Blackfoot Falls residents were generally friendly and honest, but there were always a few bad seeds in any town.

Wade immediately came to mind. No, he was just insecure and petty. And Grace had let her foolish pride open the door for him to find her Achilles' heel.

Sadie wasn't standing behind the bar like usual. Instead, she sat on a stool facing the door, a small glass of something in her hand. Looked like whiskey, though Grace had never seen the woman drink.

"Come on over here," Sadie said when Grace paused to glance around the bar.

The tables and chairs were paired and orderly, the floor swept clean. Whoever had stolen the money had left the place in good condition, so it wasn't likely revenge. But then, Sadie might've ignored the request to not touch anything.

Walking toward the older woman, Grace withdrew a small notebook from her pocket. "No forced entry from what I could see. Did you leave the bar unlocked overnight?"

"Nah. I've had the occasional bottle of whiskey go missing from time to time, and that never bothered me, but after we had that little scare a couple years back..." Sadie shrugged. "Turned out to be nothing, but I got in the habit of locking up at night."

Maybe it was nothing, maybe not. "Tell me what happened." Grace opened the notebook and clicked her pen.

Sadie frowned. "Oh, put that thing away," she said with a wave of her hand. "I only said I'd been robbed to get you over here. You want something to drink? Tonic or soda since you're on duty?"

Dumbstruck, Grace stared at her. "Sadie, you can't make false reports. It's illegal."

"For pity's sake. How else am I supposed to get you alone for a few minutes?"

"I'm serious."

"So am I."

Sighing, Grace slid onto a stool. "Is it that bad?"

"The rumors?" Sadie got to her feet and moved to the other side of the bar. "It's all Wade's doing."

"I know."

Sadie seemed surprised. "Do you know why?"

"Um, I think so." Though now Grace wasn't so sure. "Because I humiliated him yesterday?"

Chuckling, Sadie poured a soda and squeezed in some lime. "Couldn't have been too hard to do that. That boy doesn't have the brains God gave a turkey. Of course everyone knows he's bucking to be sheriff, but he also has a nephew he's hoping to hire on as deputy."

"Huh." Grace accepted the drink and took a quick sip. "No, I didn't know about that."

"So it's not enough to beat you in the election. He needs you gone so he can hire Daryl. And I can tell you for certain that boy ain't any brighter than Wade."

Grace's mouth was so dry, she gulped her soda. She wished Sadie would get back to the rumors, or Grace would have to ask outright, and she'd hate to do that.

Sadie refilled the drink, then came back around. "Here's the scuttlebutt. You were having an affair with your married partner and pressuring him to leave his wife. The two of you were arguing about it outside a store that was being robbed. He jumped out to stop the thief. You were mad and didn't back him up, and he was shot and killed."

Grace gasped. Air got trapped in her lungs, and she couldn't draw a breath. Of course, none of the account was true, all of it horrible, but that anyone could imagine her capable of allowing another human being to be gunned down made her sick to her stomach.

"I heard the same story from Marge and Louise at the diner and later from Abe at the variety store. That's pretty much it."

That was it?

Grace held in a whimper.

"Oh, honey, you're as white as a ghost," Sadie said, her eyes brimming with sympathy. "Considering the circumstances, I can't imagine Noah would mind if you had a few sips of whiskey."

"No, thank you." Her voice cracked a little. "Not while I'm on duty."

Sadie nodded and squeezed Grace's cold hand. "Folks around here can't pass up a juicy story, whether they believe it or not. But it'll die down soon enough, you'll see."

Grace silently cleared her throat. "You haven't asked me if the story's true."

"Now why would I do that when I already know the answer?" Snorting, Sadie picked up her glass. "I don't need a fancy degree to be able to read people. After listening to drunk woebegone cowboys half my life, I do just fine. And, honey," she said, gesturing with her drink at Grace. "You're no home-wrecker. And you sure ain't the type who'd sit back and watch a man die."

Sadie drained her glass and set it down with finality. "If this crap about you doesn't stop soon, I'll make up a real good yarn that'll snap up everyone's attention right quick."

Grace laughed in spite of herself. "Don't do that."

"Is it illegal? I don't think so." She stared at her empty glass. "I miss whiskey. Had to give it up on account of the diabetes. I gotta go make more tea. Stick around and have some with me." Grinning, she pushed to her feet. "Tell me how you humiliated Wade."

"I have to get back to work."

The sound of squeaky hinges had them both turning toward the door. It was Clarence.

Grace saw the scowl on his flushed face and wanted to scream. Maybe, just maybe, he'd keep things professional and not say anything until they had privacy.

"I warned you about him," he said, storming toward her. "I did. You can't say otherwise." He withdrew a white handkerchief from his royal-blue sports jacket and mopped his sweaty forehead.

"Wade?" Grace sure didn't remember him being mentioned.

"Wade? Who said anything about him?" Clarence sucked in a breath and leaned against the bar next to her. "So, you've been canoodling with him, too?"

Grace could only stare. "What are you talking about?"

"Ben…Hilda's boy. I told you right off he was trouble. That you should keep your distance. But no, you let him sniff around, and now look what's happened." He mopped his bald spot. "Sadie, get me a glass of cold water, would you, darlin'?"

Sadie folded her arms, eyes narrowed. "I'm not open yet. Get out."

His head reared back. He studied her face a second and saw she was pissed. He straightened.

"Sadie?" Grace smiled, trying with everything she had to keep her cool. "If you don't mind, I'd like to hear the mayor out."

The older woman's glare flickered. "You heard the deputy…go ahead, speak your piece."

Clarence blinked. "Now, Grace, you know it's because I care about you," he said, watching her slide the rest of her soda water toward him. "Ben Carter has always been bad news, and why you would've told him about what happened back in Arizona is beyond me." Clarence picked up the glass and drained it. "Maybe it was just pillow talk. Nothing to be ashamed of," he added quickly. "I know how you women can't help getting a little chatty during those special times…"

Sadie made the oddest noise.

Afraid Sadie was about to lunge over the bar at Clarence, Grace turned sharply.

Sadie was only trying not to laugh.

With a sigh, Grace realized she'd been kinda hoping for

a smackdown. He wanted to blame Ben? Jeez. She calmly returned her attention to Clarence. "What have you heard?"

"You want me to repeat it?"

Grace thought about it for a moment. "No, I guess that isn't necessary. Yesterday, I found out you'd told people that I left Arizona because of a bad breakup, that I was upset over being dumped."

"Not everybody. Just Noah and the deputies."

"You don't even know why I left Arizona."

"Your dad mentioned you needed a change," Clarence muttered, sounding less sure of himself. "It wasn't hard to figure out. And frankly, what I said is a whole lot better than what really happened."

"Oh, so you believe the rumors." She tried to keep her expression blank. She really hoped she'd succeeded. It shouldn't hurt that he'd accepted the gossip as gospel. This was Clarence, for heaven's sake. What did she expect?

"Look, Gracie, I didn't say we couldn't get a handle on this nonsense. Talk blows in and out of this town like the wind." He must've sensed Sadie's murderous glare and darted a nervous look at her. "This doesn't have to ruin your chance at replacing Noah. I can help you. But first you gotta promise to stay away from that Ben fella."

"Actually, no, you can't help." Grace slid off the stool, not knowing if she should laugh or cry. Clarence was her biggest obstacle to being elected. No reasonably intelligent person took him seriously. Tempted as she was to just come out and tell him that, she knew she'd regret it later.

"Good God Almighty, Clarence, you wouldn't know how to find your own ass with four hands and a mirror." Sadie snorted with disgust. "You'd best worry about your own re-election. The only reason you're still mayor is because no one else ever runs. Who knows? Maybe this year that'll change."

Clarence flushed all the way to the bald spot.

Grace knew Sadie was only trying to help, but she

shouldn't have said that. While Grace didn't need her uncle's pseudosupport, she didn't need him viewing her as a liability. Which she might have no choice about, since he was glaring at her instead of Sadie.

"By the way, Mayor..." She paused and adjusted her ball cap. "It was Wade, not Ben," she said. "Wade is responsible for the rumors.

"You know what," Sadie said, sounding suspiciously perky. "I just might run for mayor. I bet I'd get a whole lot of votes."

Grace caught the stunned look on her uncle's face just before she turned for the door. And bit her lip to keep from laughing.

At the sight of Ben, she immediately sobered.

He stood just inside the doorway. How long had he been there? Why hadn't the damn hinges squeaked? Sadie must've seen him. Why hadn't she given Grace a signal?
Jeez.

"Hey." She gave him a tentative smile, then waited for him to drag his gaze away from Clarence, who was oblivious. He'd taken Sadie's bait, and Grace could almost hear him sweat. "Come on, Ben." She tugged at his arm, hard with muscle, and was startled by how easily she could picture him stark naked. "Ben, please."

"He's an asshole," he murmured.

"Yes, he is. Let's go."

As soon as they were outside, Grace glanced down both sides of Main Street. Fewer people were out and about than earlier. The others were no doubt gathered at the diner, gossiping about her. "How did you know I was at The Watering Hole?"

"I saw your truck. And you weren't in the diner or the office, so I figured I'd check the bar."

"You didn't happen to see Wade, did you?"

"Did you hear him screaming like a little girl? Are my knuckles bloodied?"

"Ben." She gave him a stern look.

He smiled. "You look cute in that ball cap."

"Cute?" She sighed. "Not what I was going for," she said, then got nervous when he glanced around. She knew exactly what he was thinking, because she wanted to kiss him, too. "I'm still on duty. Okay?" The way his gaze fixed on her mouth sent excitement zinging through her veins. Damn him. "Nod once if you understand."

Nearby laughter drew her attention. Two older women she knew only by sight had just walked out of the fabric store across the street. The second they saw her, they exchanged glances.

"I came by last night," Ben said. "I knocked."

"Did you?" She saw the speculation in his eyes and had to look away. "I don't feel comfortable standing out here. Lots of talk making the rounds."

He waited for her to look at him again. "It'll die down."

"I know. Sadie said the same thing." Grace started for her truck with Ben beside her. "In the meantime—"

"You're coming with me to the Sundance tonight."

Grace shook her head, trying to ignore the dilapidated green pickup that had slowed down. The elderly driver stared openly at her. She'd never seen him before. Judging by the load of supplies he was hauling, he didn't visit town often. And yet he'd already heard?

"Come on, it'll do you good to get away from here. Mom's cooking Mexican food…homemade tortillas and everything."

"Look, I'm a big girl," Grace said, her paranoia growing. What foolishness. She was still new to the area and the first woman deputy, so there would be stares no matter what. "I'll be fine. Spend time with your mom."

"She specifically invited you."

A cowboy leaving the barber shop was busy brushing off his shoulders until he spotted Grace. He did a double-take just as Ben's words sunk in.

She looked at him. "Why would she invite me?"

"Good question," he muttered. "Now that I think about it."

"You're still leaving day after tomorrow, right?" She held her breath waiting for his answer. Stupid. Very stupid.

He nodded, his gaze lowering to her mouth. "You don't belong here." His unexpected remark stunned her.

Not that she hadn't thought the same thing a hundred times. "What happened to the pep talk?"

"Hell, you can do this job with your eyes closed. But you'll be bored. You need diversity, the challenge a big city can offer."

She couldn't think about that. If the rumors didn't sink her, she couldn't afford to write off this move as a mistake. Things hadn't died down in Arizona so her options were limited. Ben knew that, so there was nothing for her to say.

They walked in silence to her truck. She'd initially planned on stopping in the office but reconsidered.

"People bad-mouth LA," Ben said as if there'd been no gap in the conversation. "But there are some nice outlying areas."

Startled, her hand paused on the door handle. He seemed a bit uncomfortable. Probably just realized how that sounded. "I told you, I'm over the whole Disneyland thing."

He smiled. "Tonight. I'll come get you at five," he said, and when she opened her mouth to object, he added, "Get in the truck, Grace, or I'll kiss you in front of the whole damn town."

18

DINNER AT THE Sundance wasn't just dinner. It was an event, an experience all by itself. Loud, exuberant and wonderful. Crazy as the thought seemed, Grace never knew families like this existed. There were no rules or expectations. With maybe one exception. Grace got the feeling that if Hilda set a sampler plate in front of you, you didn't dare refuse.

"What did you think of the chile relleno?" Jamie asked. She and Cole were sitting across the table from Grace and Ben.

Grace liked Jamie, despite the fact that her eyes were sparkling with mischief. Probably because the dish was so spicy, it about blew the top of Grace's head off. "It was...good."

Everyone laughed.

Thankfully, Hilda and Barbara had just disappeared into the kitchen.

"Want another helping?" Rachel asked as she rose from the table.

Grace whimpered softly.

Chuckling, Ben slid an arm along the back of her chair and whispered, "Don't worry, you won't hurt my mom's feelings."

Her cheeks heated as his warm breath caressed her face.

Ben had been circumspect, which she appreciated, but when he was this close, he wasn't the problem. She wanted to lean into him, to feel his arms around her.

She shifted her gaze and moved just far enough that she wouldn't feel his heat. And found herself looking at her boss. Thankfully, he was busy talking to Jesse.

Noah was the only other person here who wasn't *family*. A heads-up that he was coming would've been nice. Though Ben hadn't known in advance, either. But that didn't solve the problem of whether she should say something to Noah about the rumors. It wasn't the time or place, but she'd never have a better opportunity.

"Don't listen to Rachel," Trace said as he tried to pass his sister his plate. "She gets grumpy when it's her night to do dishes."

"Yeah, like I'm going to fall for that." Rachel grabbed two empty pitchers and muttered, "I don't even live here anymore, you moron," before she pushed through the swinging door to the kitchen.

Ben let out a loud laugh. "Fifteen years and you two are still at it."

Overwhelming agreement was expressed around the huge table that sat eleven of them quite comfortably. Nikki, Trace's fiancée, was working at The Watering Hole, and Rachel's husband, Matt, was away on business. The only people Grace hadn't really spoken to were Jesse and his fiancée, Shea, because they were seated at the other end of the table.

Barbara poked her head in from the kitchen. "Are we ready?"

Trace muttered a curse. "Just a minute, Mom," he said while he scrambled to gather the dirty plates.

Grace got up to help, but Ben touched her arm. "It's okay," he said. "We have a system."

He stacked their plates on the empty serving platters in front of them, then passed everything down the line to

Trace. Everyone seemed to know the drill. In seconds, the table was clear.

Barbara had lingered in the doorway, her pleased smile aimed at Ben and then extending to Grace before she disappeared. It seemed that everyone was glad to have him back in the fold. Tonight was like reliving old times, and they hadn't pulled any punches when it came to childhood stories about him. But it was all in good fun.

Trace got rid of the dishes they'd collected. Then Hilda and Barbara carried in carafes of coffee. Rachel followed behind them, balancing a cake that she set carefully on the table in front of Noah.

It was shaped like a gold marshal's star with red lettering that Grace couldn't make out from where she sat.

Noah stared at it a moment. "You are three of the most hardheaded women I've ever known," he said, shaking his head. "I asked you very nicely not to make a big deal out of me leaving."

"We canceled the party, didn't we?" Rachel glared at him. "Damn killjoy."

Ben leaned over for a better look at the writing. "I know who made the cake." He grinned at Rachel. "You spelled *'hasta luego'* wrong."

"I'm so glad you were here to point that out." With a sniff, she turned to Noah. "I started to write *'adios,'* but I just couldn't. I love Alana. I love seeing the two of you together, but I hate that you're leaving. We finally have Ben back and now you're…" Rachel's voice cracked.

"Ah, come on, it's not as if I won't be coming home to visit," Noah said, pushing back in his chair. "You'll see more of me than when I was in the army."

Grace glanced at Ben to see his reaction to Rachel. After all, he was only visiting. When his expression remained eerily blank, she risked a peek at Hilda. She was also focused on Ben.

"Hell, Rach," Trace said, frowning at her. "You pregnant or something?"

She blinked at him. A single tear fell, and she dabbed furiously at it. "You're such a jerk, you know that? I have no idea what Nikki sees in you."

"What?" Trace seemed genuinely perplexed and looked around for support. "She's getting all emotional. What am I supposed to think?"

His brothers were shaking their heads and trying not to laugh. Noah had pulled Rachel into a hug while giving Trace a deadpan look over her head.

With a collective sigh, Barbara, Hilda and Jamie started pouring coffee.

"I'm getting a beer," Trace said. "Anyone else?"

Turned out all the guys wanted beer, so Noah went with him to the kitchen. And Rachel got to work cutting the cake.

Grace's offer of help was politely refused just as it had been earlier.

Ben seemed lost in thought until Cole asked him a question about a pair of chestnut colts. Only then did she realize Ben had been staring at her. She met his gaze, and he smiled before turning to answer Cole.

She didn't mind them discussing business. They'd talked before dinner about the type of stock Ben would be purchasing and the most efficient means of transportation. She liked listening to them, but mostly she loved hearing the excitement Ben couldn't keep out of his voice. He desperately wanted to help the McAllisters, even if he wouldn't admit it. The satisfaction of giving back would go a long way toward healing old hurts.

What bothered her was her own foolish heart. Just because Ben might be making trips back to check out stock had nothing to do with her. She'd be an idiot to get her hopes up. Sure, he'd probably call her when he was in town.

But that was it. He'd be coming for business purposes and to see his mom. Not to see Grace.

She felt a slight squeeze on her thigh and smiled. Ben had reached under the table while talking to Cole. She was about to return the favor when Hilda set a mug of coffee in front of her.

Grace leaned back and moved her leg. "Thank you."

"You want cream?" Hilda asked, her eyes bright with amusement. So she'd seen them playing under the table.

"Black is fine."

Hilda surprised her by taking the vacated seat next to Grace. "So, you've been living here for three weeks?" She spoke with little accent.

"Pretty close."

"You like Blackfoot Falls?"

Grace hesitated. "It's different from Arizona, but I'm getting used to it."

"I had trouble when I first arrived," Hilda said. "But that was many years ago."

Grace nodded, then worried she'd given away too much when curiosity narrowed Hilda's gaze. Was she wondering how much Ben had told Grace?

She smiled and leaned close. "I was hoping my son would find a nice girl here. And a sheriff, too."

"Oh, no. We…" Grace stammered. "Um…"

Rachel leaned between them and set two pieces of cake on the table. With a wink at Grace, Rachel inclined her head at Hilda. "Is she planning your wedding yet?"

The older woman snorted at Rachel. "This one was more trouble to raise than all four of the boys."

Just when Grace decided to slide under the table and crawl to the door, Ben turned to them. He lifted his brows at Rachel. "And here I've always blamed Trace for being the troublemaker."

"Oh, he is. I'm just better at getting away with it," she said and grinned at Grace before moving on.

Okay, they were joking.

Grace hoped. Ben hadn't actually smiled. And this wasn't the first time someone implied they were a couple. All Grace needed were more rumors to circulate. About how she would pine away over Ben once he left. She trusted the McAllisters would never spread gossip, but sometimes jokes had a way of becoming overblown.

Trace and Noah returned, loaded with six-packs of beer. They took them straight to the wet bar in the den, where, according to Ben, everyone tended to congregate to talk or play pool.

After the cake was eaten and cleanup was done, sure enough, there was a migration to the den. Cole had another question for Ben, and Grace saw Noah standing alone. She was trying to decide whether to approach him when Trace came from the back.

"Come on, Sheriff." He motioned with his beer. "I might as well beat you first and get it over with."

Noah snorted a laugh. "In a minute," he said, glancing briefly at Grace before telling Trace, "I'd better make it twenty. You need the practice."

Trace had a choice word for him before heading to the back.

"Grace, you mind if we talk business for a few minutes?"

Her stomach lurched. This was the opportunity she wanted, but it wouldn't be easy. "I was hoping we'd have a chance to talk."

He glanced around. Cole and Ben were still in the dining room. Rachel and Jamie were returning china to the hutch. Noah gestured to the empty living room. "I won't keep you long."

"I wanted to say something earlier," she began. "About the rumors going around town. They aren't true."

"I know that."

Grace blinked. The man was ace at keeping his face

blank. But then she saw the momentary disgust in his eyes. "It's Wade. You showed him up, and he's steamed."

She stared at the gleaming hardwood floor. "I'm partly to blame. I wasn't just showing him up...I was showing off."

"I heard about that fancy shooting."

She looked up. "How?"

"Danny can't stop talking about it."

Grace winced. "Great." That ought to keep Wade foaming at the mouth. "I screwed up. I shouldn't have—"

"When I offered to cover the phones while the four of you went to the range, you think I didn't know what would happen? Granted, I was hoping that seeing you in action would shut Wade up. I pegged that wrong."

Grace frowned. "Why did you think—" She paused to organize her thoughts. Glen from Internal Affairs had crafted a nice, tidy exit profile for her file, geared toward qualifying her for this job. So as not to raise questions about why she'd accept a job as a small-town deputy, it played down her task force role and commendations for marksmanship. "What do you know about—"

"I know enough," he said with quiet certainty. "I had a word with Wade, and he won't be shooting his mouth off anymore. Unfortunately, what's already making the rounds, I have no control over. Trust me, Grace, you have people in your corner. You can weather this crap."

"You mean Clarence?"

Noah laughed—whether at the suggestion or her just-shoot-me expression, she wasn't sure.

"Okay." She still wanted to know what Noah had dug up on her. His information hadn't come from Ben. No way she'd believe that. She glanced over her shoulder. Cole was gone, and Ben was focused on his phone. He didn't seem particularly happy. In fact, he looked worried.

"Grace?"

She turned back to Noah. "Sorry."

"I wish I could do more about this mess. Mainly, I don't want this thing with Wade to discourage you from staying. Blackfoot Falls needs someone like you."

Was he kidding? She still hadn't figured out how he'd lasted this long. She managed to smile.

Noah did, too. "You think you'll be bored out of your mind." He shrugged. "Maybe. It all depends on how much you want to put into the job. More happens in this corner of Montana than most people realize."

Grace leaned a bit closer. "I'm listening."

"I can't say much now. Only that the BLM people are understaffed and fighting a losing battle. Not only with poachers. You should know the Fish and Wildlife warden is very impressed with you."

"I don't see how. I called them too late."

"Joe Hardy and I go way back. He knows enough about Wade and Roy that he wouldn't expect them to lift a finger. But here you come, new, unfamiliar with the foothills, and you charge right in. BLM agents cover a lot of territory. You had a much better chance of nailing the poachers. Joe always appreciates help from the surrounding counties."

"I can imagine."

"It's more than that, though," Noah said. "Blackfoot Falls, hell, the whole county, is growing."

"Hey, are you two talking business? It's not allowed." Carrying beer and a bottle of wine, Rachel stopped on her way to the back. "Where's Ben? Did the wedding planning scare him off?"

"Right behind you, big mouth." Despite his teasing, Ben didn't appear to be in a good mood.

Grace had lost track of him for a while, and she hoped it was a text or phone call that was bothering him. Not the jokes or the sly looks. Even his mother's well-intentioned comments could be getting on his nerves.

Rachel exchanged Noah's empty bottle for a full one,

then offered a beer to Ben. But he shook his head. Grace hung on to her iced tea.

"In all seriousness," Rachel said, "it's good to have you here, Grace. A woman sheriff in Blackfoot Hills is awesome all by itself, but—"

Grace shook her head. "You know I'm a deputy."

"Okay, but surely you'll be taking Noah's place." Rachel looked to him for confirmation. "I mean, come on... who else? Wade? Roy? Please."

"Excuse me, ladies," Noah said. "I'm gonna go shoot some pool."

Rachel sighed with frustration. She started to follow him, then glanced back at Grace. "We really do need you here. Noah has spoiled all of us. He elevated the office to a new level."

Grace watched her go, then turned to Ben, who hadn't lost his preoccupied frown. "Is something wrong?"

"I don't know," he said, a distant look in his eyes. "Maybe."

She couldn't tell if it was from anger, fear or concern.

"You mind cutting this short?" he asked.

"No. Of course not."

"Let's go say good-night." He gestured for her to go ahead of him.

She expected to feel his hand on her back. Or even a light brushing of their arms. But he didn't touch her. Didn't say another word all the way to the den.

The room was huge with a stone fireplace, two couches and club chairs on one side, the pool table and wet bar on the other. Trace and Jesse were playing, while Noah, Cole and Jamie sipped beers and watched. Shea and Barbara sat in front of the fireplace, laughing at something Rachel said.

Hilda walked up behind Grace.

"Mom. Good." Ben stepped aside to let her pass. "Everyone's here. Sorry for the interruption, folks," he said, and waited a second. "Something's come up. I have to leave."

"Oh, Benedicto, no." Hilda grasped his hand. "Just a while longer."

"I'm sorry, Mom," he said, shaking his head. "I have to drive back to LA first thing tomorrow."

There was a chorus of groans.

But no one was more stunned than Grace.

THEY WERE HALFWAY to town before Ben realized that Grace had barely said anything. He'd been too distracted to notice. Hell, he'd spent most of the evening wrapped up in his own head. Dinner should've been a nice, relaxing way for Grace to get to know his mom and the McAllisters.

Goddamn Lena.

First it was the jumbled text, then an hour later, her raging phone call. He hoped she was just drunk and not doing coke with that young bartender from the club on Sunset. The guy was trouble. He knew just how to play to vain older women.

"I'm sorry about tonight," he said, dividing his attention between Grace and the road.

"No need to apologize. Business is business. If there'd been an emergency, Noah and I would've left in a heartbeat." She didn't sound angry or even disappointed. She didn't sound like anything. That was the problem. "You should've pulled your mom aside and told her privately."

Ah, okay.

Ben smiled. Grace didn't use sweet-talk or tears to get her way. She spoke her mind, even to tell him something he might not want to hear. He wasn't used to that. He hadn't figured out if he liked it.

"You're right." He reached for her hand. "I should've told you privately, too."

"No, you don't owe me anything."

"Grace."

"We're good, okay?"

Her hand tensed, and he let it go. "Funny, I was just thinking about how refreshing it is that you don't play games."

She turned sharply to him. "I don't. What's your point?"

"You're mad. And I'm not saying you don't have that right. It's that you won't admit it."

She exhaled a deep breath. "I'm not mad. I'm sad you're leaving. It doesn't matter that I knew the day was coming, I'll still miss you." She leaned her head back and slid down a few inches. "You and Sadie are my only two friends here."

Ben chuckled.

"What?"

"Sadie and me, huh? I thought I might rate a slightly higher ranking."

"Oh, for God's sake...I can give myself an orgasm."

Ben laughed so loud he didn't hear his phone ring. Grace had to tell him.

It was Lena again. Of course. He ignored the call. Nothing he said would matter at this point. He hoped her threats were hollow, forgotten by the time she sobered up. The best he could do was be in LA by Monday when the bank opened. Once they closed on the ranch, he didn't care what Lena got herself into.

"It's my partner," he said as they came upon Main Street. "She's being difficult."

"You're still getting your ranch, though. Aren't you?"

"One way or another." He smiled, hoping to chase the worry from her face. "I overheard some of what you and Noah were talking about. Sounded as if he was giving you a pep talk."

"He doesn't want me to assume all is lost, or that I'll be bored."

Ben nodded. He'd heard more than he let on. Selfishly,

he hoped she would decide small-town living wasn't for her. Damn, he wasn't ready to leave her yet.

He pulled into The Boarding House's lot and parked the Porsche in his usual spot, away from the other cars. The light from the porch illuminated Grace's face. She gave him a sweet smile.

"I have to leave early tomorrow," he said. "Really early."

Her gaze flickered. "I know."

They got out of the car and, hand in hand, walked in silence to her room.

She let them in and without speaking they pulled the bed covers down, got undressed and slipped between the sheets. He pulled her close and soaked in her warmth. Underneath the beautiful face and silky skin, Grace was a rock. And to think he'd had to come all the way back home to find her.

"You need to sleep," she whispered, and he kissed her until only her soft, breathy moans filled the room.

19

THE DAY AFTER Ben left, Grace decided to spend her day off in bed. She wasn't moping. That wasn't in her nature. She simply needed to allow herself the time and means to grieve.

She missed him. There was no way around it. And why wouldn't she? Against her better judgment, she'd taken that headlong plunge into love. A month ago, she wouldn't have believed it possible. But a closer look at the week they'd spent together convinced her it wasn't so surprising. She'd always been attracted to strong, confident men. But a man with those qualities who could admit his faults *and* be willing to own up to his mistakes?

Come on, of course she was toast. It made perfect sense. But she couldn't help wishing she'd never come to Blackfoot Falls. That she'd never met Ben. Because now it hurt like hell.

After brushing her teeth, she slid back in between the sheets. Despite all the assurances, the gossip hadn't died down. If anything, things had gotten worse, mostly because Sadie had publicly declared her intention to run for mayor in the November election.

The announcement had everyone speculating that the rumors about Grace had to be true, and that poor Clarence was giving up hope of reelection after being duped by his own scandalous niece. Sadie had tried to straighten things out, but even with Marge's help, word had continued to spread. The amount of sympathy for Clarence was almost comical.

The only upside was that he was keeping his distance.

Grace rearranged her pillow and listened to the morning traffic on Main Street, which consisted of four trucks, maybe five? She glanced at the alarm clock…then at her phone sitting in the charger.

Ben should've arrived in LA by now. But she didn't know for sure, because she hadn't heard from him since the voice mail he'd left last night. Unfortunately, she'd been in the shower, but he'd let her know he was halfway to LA and had stopped for a few hours' sleep. He'd sounded tired and edgy, and she'd wanted like crazy to call him back. But she would've risked waking him.

She'd assumed he would try her again before he got on the road. But he hadn't, which wasn't like him. Or maybe it was. Right now, she wasn't sure of anything. She'd given in and called him earlier, but had been sent straight to voice mail.

She'd known he was upset before he left, something about his business partner being horrible, but he hadn't wanted to talk about it. She hadn't pushed.

When they'd returned from the Sundance, he'd been wonderful. Their bittersweet time together had been all about deep, slow kisses and tender touches. Sadly, she'd had to cut things short knowing he had twenty hours of driving ahead of him. He hadn't argued. Just kissed her and held her in his arms until she'd dozed off.

Her hand ran over "his" side of the bed. It was still as empty and cold as the morning she'd woken up to find him gone.

Yes, she'd known he would be leaving early…

But not to wake her and say goodbye?

It still hurt. She suspected it would continue to hurt for a long while.

At least she didn't have to go into the office today and see Wade's stupid, smug face. That was something.

God, her life was pathetic.

THE NEXT DAY, Noah asked Grace to come in thirty minutes early, so she grabbed a Danish from the table in the lobby and walked straight to the office.

She opened the door, and Noah looked up from the coffee he was pouring. "Want some?"

"Sure. Thanks." She smiled when he passed her a mug of the dark brew. Industrial strength, she liked to call it.

"Admit it," he said, "you're going to miss my coffee."

She blinked. He was firing her? She sighed, realizing he meant he'd be gone in a week. "I'm going to miss you, Sheriff. I would've enjoyed working for you."

He studied her a moment. "You'll like being the person calling the shots even more."

Well, she was pretty sure Noah wasn't delusional, but damn close if he still thought she'd be elected sheriff. He sat behind his desk, and she turned a chair to face him.

She doubted he'd taken his gaze off her once. "You might be too far removed from the grapevine, but talk has—"

Noah laughed. "Nobody is exempt in this town, including me. Though it helps to remind these good people that I carry a gun. You might keep that tip in mind."

Grace smiled. Smart, good-looking, great sense of humor... She wondered how many hearts Noah had broken when he'd fallen for a Sundance guest. Of course, Ben had all those qualities and more. But he wasn't hers.

"I trust Ben made it to LA okay?"

She blinked. "I assume so."

Noah frowned. His stare lingered past the point of rudeness, then shifted to the window. Clearly deep in thought, it took him a while to get back to the conversation. "I know it's been tough. Sometimes rumors take on a life of their own. Roy and Danny have been putting out fires here and there, but with Sadie getting in the mix—"

"Roy and Danny?"

"They feel badly about what's happening. They aren't happy with Wade playing dirty."

"Huh." Their support made a difference. Though at this point, a very small one.

"I want to name you acting sheriff, Grace, but first I need to know you're planning to stay."

Now it was her turn to stare. This she had not expected. "What about Clarence?"

"Don't worry about him."

She knew her uncle had a say, but her bet was on Noah, who was well respected. He'd said not to worry and she wouldn't, even though Noah would be long gone by November. "You're taking a big chance on me."

"The hell I am." He let out a short laugh. "Now if Wade were the only candidate, that would make me nervous." He leaned back, looking serious again. "I'm gonna say something that's none of my business, but seeing you and Ben together— I gotta wonder if you'll be happy here."

"I don't follow."

"I know Ben. We literally grew up together. And after seeing you two, I know he'll try to convince you to join him in LA. Law enforcement is a lot more exciting out there."

"What? That's crazy. We just met. We're barely friends…"

Noah's small smile indicated he thought otherwise. "Look, I don't want to interfere. I just need to know how hard I should fight for you. I owe this place a decent sheriff. Even if I have to find one myself."

Why was she hesitating? With Noah going to bat for her, of course she should give Blackfoot Falls another shot. Noah himself had lit a fire under her when he'd told her about what the job could be and, apparently Roy and Danny didn't hate her.

Ben should have nothing to do with her decision. Nothing at all. Anyway, Noah was wrong. He'd known Ben once, but not now. "Will you give me until the end of the day?"

"Tomorrow afternoon is fine." Noah smiled. "I'm glad you haven't given up on the town. These people need you."

"Thanks." She glanced at the clock. Almost time to start her shift. Just as she rose, the door opened.

It was Wade. Crossing the threshold and giving them both an evil look.

She grabbed the truck keys and brushed past him, although his pure hatred clung like an afterimage from staring at the sun. She needed air. And some coffee that wouldn't eat through her stomach lining.

FROM HIS HOUSE in Valencia, Ben drove to Lena's place, bleary-eyed and pissed. He'd made it home around 5:00 a.m. and gotten a few hours of sleep. But the ten hours before had been brutal.

First, massive freeway delays had slowed him down, and then he'd broken his phone six hours outside LA. He'd stopped for coffee and made the mistake of checking his texts. Lena's bullshit had made him angry, something about her changing their contract. He'd slammed his phone down so hard, it had shattered. He'd wanted to call Grace. She would have calmed him down. But he would've woken her. And anyway, he had no damn phone.

So of course he'd gotten up early, bought a new one and had it synced.

Lena owned a place in Coldwater Canyon where it met Mulholland Drive, beautiful and private, if you didn't mind a forty-five minute drive to and from the valley. Naturally, she didn't answer the door. Some ripped dude without a shirt told Ben she was by the pool.

He stepped onto the deck, then made his way to the lounge area—basically, Lena's throne room.

"Where the hell have you been?" She was dressed impeccably as always, this time in a tight beige skirt, a white blouse and five-inch heels. "It's about time." She shook back her perfectly styled blond hair. "Don't you dare ignore my texts. Do you hear me? I won't stand for—"

"Stop it, Lena."

Surprisingly, she did.

"My phone broke. I had to buy a new one this morning."

"You never heard of a public phone?"

"Look, I'm tired, starving and pissed about my phone, so can we just get down to business?"

She crossed her arms. "I'm not sure. I don't like dealing with you when you're all pissy."

He laughed out loud. When he finished, he turned one of the patio chairs around and sat down. He was tempted to dive into her infinity pool, but Lena sounded lucid, and he wanted to get this done.

"What's this about you changing the contract?" he asked. "The contract we agreed upon six months ago. The contract your lawyer drew up. What could you possibly want changed at the eleventh hour?"

"Something I should have done from the beginning."

He knew that tone of voice. He'd expected it. Whenever she did something underhanded, she sounded even snippier than usual.

"Okay," he said when she didn't spit it out. "What's the change?"

"There's a copy of the contract on the table." She nodded to an envelope behind him.

"Lena, come on. Just tell me."

She didn't respond right away, as expected, and he knew she was glaring, though he couldn't see her eyes behind her sunglasses. Lena Graves was a beautiful woman well into her forties. Her figure was sculpted by private trainers and she had a gorgeous face to go with it. She was also a savvy businesswoman who used everything in her arsenal to get her way.

"We changed the split," she said, as if it was an afterthought that he was still there. "It's now fifty-one/forty-nine."

Ben stood. "That better be in my favor."

"Of course it's not in your favor. Why should it be? I'm the one with the most to lose. It's my money on the line. All you have to do is play with horses all day. I don't see why you should get an equal share when our contributions aren't equal."

For a moment, anger paralyzed him.

Instead of tipping over her goddamn patio table, Ben stared out at the San Fernando Valley. Well, at what was hiding the valley, because from up here, all he really saw was smog.

Then he took a look at the eastern view. On a clear day, he could see the Hollywood Bowl Amphitheater, downtown Los Angeles and out to the ocean and Catalina Island. He wondered if there'd ever be a clear day in Los Angeles again.

Funny how difficult it was to see the smog when he was in the thick of it. He had had to step away for that.

Something clicked inside him, and he saw his own life split in two. On one side, his dream Ventura ranch, working with the contacts he'd made in the past twelve years, working with Lena and all the other folks like her. Talk about swimming with sharks. There was no town more vicious except for Washington, DC.

On the other side: Grace.

"I suppose you're angry now," Lena said. "But I've talked to—"

"You know what?" he said, not giving a damn about what she was saying. "I'm done."

"What do you mean, done?" She actually stood. "Done with what?"

"With everything."

"You're not planning to—what do you mean...everything?"

He shook his head, laughing as he turned to go. He didn't feel any goodbyes were needed.

Not even after she called after him. "Fine. We'll make it fifty/fifty."

It might be smoggy as hell, but Ben had never seen things so clearly. He wasn't sure what he was going to do yet, but it wouldn't include anymore of this backstabbing bullshit.

GRACE WENT STRAIGHT to her room after her shift ended. Before she stripped off her uniform shirt and jeans, she pulled out the list she'd stuck in her back pocket. It was difficult to read her scrawl because the paper had been folded so many times. And then there was more doodling than actual helpful items in either the pro or con column.

She'd jotted down things throughout the day as they came to her. That is, when she was able to keep her mind off Ben.

Another thought registered as she put on her red T-shirt and yoga pants. She had no winter clothes. Well, not the kind she'd need here. That would cost her. Definitely a con.

She spread her paper on the small table, grabbed a cold soda and a pen, then sat. She stared at the pros. Noah believed in her. She'd be in charge. More money. She'd started making friends. She'd get to fire Wade!—that was a biggie. Roy and Danny were fed up with Wade. Sadie could be mayor in November. The chances of having another opportunity like this again were very slim. Any other place would be just as hard to get used to.

Ben would be back.

She took a big swig of her soda and quickly switched to the cons. She might lose in November. Clarence. Wade. Small-town gossip. Winter. Being the first woman at anything was a risk. Her, sheriff in a cowboy town? Roy and Danny would have to be retrained.

Ben would be back.

She ran her hands through her hair. She'd already known the pros were greater than the cons. But she needed more time to think.

Noah was being great, and she knew he'd get her up to speed quickly if she said yes. A lot of people would think she got the position because she was friendly with the McAllisters, or because Ben was a friend of Noah's. But she wasn't going to make this decision based on emotion. If she did, she might as well just throw in the towel now.

But it wasn't as if she could flip a switch and stop thinking about Ben. She couldn't pretend that she hadn't fallen for him or that it didn't hurt. And when he came back to see his mom—

Her phone rang, and she forced herself to stop hoping it was Ben.

She picked it up and blinked at the screen. Hard.

Holy crap. It was Ben.

Grace let it ring three times while she collected herself, then answered, "Hey."

"Am I catching you at a good time?" He sounded tired.

"Yeah."

"I'm sorry for not calling again. This trip hasn't exactly gone to plan. I broke my phone in the middle of the night, and when I got home, I crashed hard."

His phone broke? Really? Maybe his dog ate his homework, too. "You're there and safe, so...that's what counts."

"How's it going with the rumors?"

Her heart sank with each beat. No "I missed you" or anything even remotely personal. God, she was being foolish. "It's nothing I can't ride out. What happened with the loan?"

He paused. "It fell through. But I'm not making that public yet, so..."

"Got it. Secret. No problem."

Silence stretched between them.

Had her voice betrayed her disappointment? Surely, it must have. Until he'd left, she hadn't realized how deeply she'd wanted this thing with Ben to be real. To be more. But that was no reason to act cold. "I'm really sorry about the ranch."

"It's not the end. Just a bump in the road."

Okay. That made the picture pretty clear. He was back in his element with his real priorities. He probably regretted telling her so much about himself. "So what do you plan do to next?"

"Not sure. Other than more stunt work. There's a film coming up... I don't know. I'm too exhausted to think straight."

She winced, as if closing her eyes would change the fact that this whole conversation was awkward. Somehow that was the worst part. "Well, it sounds like you should get some more sleep."

"Yeah," he said, his voice distant. "I'll call you later, okay?"

"Sure," she said, and disconnected the call, wishing she could wipe out the past five minutes.

The man she'd just spoken to...he wasn't the Ben she knew, and it hurt. She wasn't sorry for telling him about Arizona. Although she'd be more careful about that kind of thing in the future. But at least she didn't tell him about Noah's offer or that she'd have to give her answer tomorrow. Neither of which provided much solace. She curled up on her bed and didn't even try to stop crying.

BEN STARED BLINDLY at the calendar on his desk, wishing he could take back everything he'd said to Grace. But he hadn't wanted to tell her the whole story, not when he was so beat and raw with disappointment. And yeah, somewhat embarrassed. Not that he wouldn't tell her. He'd walked away from his dream today without having a plan B, except to keep knocking on doors until he found another investor. Or saved the money himself. But that would take forever.

The hard work didn't discourage him. Being in this town did. Hell, he'd fought long and hard to become an in-demand stunt man. But LA had never been less appealing. Not after his trip to Montana. Not after Grace.

He slumped back in his chair, wishing she were here to help him think this through.

His cell rang in his hand. When he saw the name on the screen, he frowned. Why would Rachel call him now?

GRACE HAD GONE to work with puffy, red eyes, but no one had remarked on it, not even Wade. She'd gone in early to tell Noah her decision. He'd accepted it with no fuss, and she'd gone on about her thrilling duty of preparing paperwork for the county commissioner's office, mostly reports of tickets.

She'd picked up a ready-made salad at the store for lunch, and now she was cleaning out the back of the truck. She'd been putting it off, annoyed at Gus's and Danny's sloppiness. Sharing a vehicle sucked.

A car parked right behind her, and she clenched her teeth. There were empty spaces up and down the block. It was just some little white compact. It could fit anywhere. But she wasn't going to blow it out of proportion just because she was down in the dumps. She was almost done clearing out Danny's garbage, anyway.

But when a guy stepped up all in her space, she swiveled around in a huff. "Can I help—"

"Yeah," Ben said, taking hold of her arms, keeping her still. "I'm pretty sure you're the only one who can help."

"What? How?" It really was Ben. Disheveled and gorgeous even with three days' growth of beard. "What are you doing here? How did you even get here?"

"I flew to Kalispell."

Her mouth fell open. All she could think of was his red Porsche.

"On an airplane," he said. "I didn't grow wings."

"What?" She blinked at the small white compact. "Why?"

"So I could catch you before you left. So I could tell you I'm sorry for that stupid phone call and for anything else I've done that may have given you the impression you didn't matter to me."

His hands were kind of tight, but that was okay. She had the feeling she wouldn't be steady on her own. Not with what he was saying...

This had better not be a dream.

No, she could feel his grip, his heat. Could see the warmth in his hazel eyes.

"I realized when I went to meet Lena that I didn't want to be in Hollywood anymore. Not that I don't still want a ranch. Do you know how many movies and TV shows are filmed in this part of the country? A lot." He shrugged his broad shoulders and smiled that perfect smile of his. "But that's not the point."

Grace was grinning, too. "Have you slept at all since we talked?"

"A couple hours maybe. Not many flights go to Kalispell. And none of them direct." He touched her cheek. "When Rachel told me you were leaving town, I did what I had to do to catch you."

"Rachel?" But...she knew better. Grace noticed her standing between Sadie and Nikki on the sidewalk in front of the bar, all of them looking happy and weepy at the same time. Those little devils...

Ben exhaled a deep, shuddering breath. "I know it seems too soon, I guess, since I've never felt this way before." He swallowed. "I'm in love with you, Grace. And I think you might come to love me if you give me a chance. I know you're leaving, and that's okay, because I'll go wherever you want to go. I still have some money. I'll sell the Porsche, my Valencia house. I've been thinking it over while waiting for planes and sitting on flights. California is expensive. I don't want to live there anymore. I can find an affordable ranch almost anywhere else." He paused. "Whatever you want, Grace."

She wasn't sure she could respond. She had the words, but he'd stolen her breath away. He loved her. Enough to race back to Blackfoot Falls. And he respected her, enough to follow wherever her career took her. Above all that, though, was the way he was looking at her. She could see it. The love that she'd seen in her own mirror when she thought of him. "Oh, you poor, exhausted man. I won't need time to fall in love with you. I'm already there."

Ben loosened his grip on her slowly, as if her words were easing his desperation bit by bit. "You love me?"

She nodded. "I do. And I want to get to know everything about you."

"I was thinking the very same thing."

"On the plane?"

"Nope. That was on the drive to California. You were never far from my thoughts, Grace. I woke up thinking about how I'd left you without saying goodbye. I'm sorry for that. You looked so peaceful and beautiful as you slept that disturbing you didn't seem right." His gaze shifted from her eyes, but only for a second. "Are you on duty?"

She nodded.

"Have any time left on your break?"

Grace looked at her watch, her head spinning with all he'd said. "Nine minutes."

"How about we go to your room?"

Now she noticed the crowd they were attracting. "We'll have to be fast."

He took her hand, and they walked as quickly as possible, just under a jog, to The Boarding House. She managed to open her door in one try, and then it was just the two of them.

Ben kissed her, and it was unlike any other kiss…except for the kiss by the stream. Was that when she'd fallen in love?

He drew back, and she was about to complain when he said, "So, where are we going?"

He didn't know. She hadn't told him or anyone else that she'd accepted Noah's offer. She pulled him closer. "How does right here in Blackfoot Falls sound?"

"Does that mean I'm kissing the Sheriff of Blackfoot Falls?"

"Not yet. Noah will make the announcement soon. But remember, it's only temporary. I could lose the election in November."

"I'll take that chance and start looking for some land." He smiled, shaking his head. "I don't understand how giving up pretty much everything is giving me more than I ever dreamed." He tilted her chin up. "Congratulations, Sheriff Hendrix." Then he kissed her.

And Grace knew this was the start of her brand-new life.

* * * * *

#839 WICKED SECRETS
Uniformly Hot!
by Anne Marsh
When Navy rescue swimmer Tag Johnson commands their one-night stand turn into a fake engagement, former Master Sergeant Mia Brandt doesn't know whether to refuse...or follow orders!

#840 THE MIGHTY QUINNS: ELI
The Mighty Quinns
by Kate Hoffmann
For a reality TV show, Lucy Parker must live in a remote cabin with no help. Search and rescue expert Eli Montgomery tempts Lucy with his wilderness skills—and his body. Accepting jeopardizes her job...and her defenses.

#841 GOOD WITH HIS HANDS
The Wrong Bed
by Tanya Michaels
Danica Yates just wants a hot night with the sexy architect in her building to help her forget her would-be wedding. She's shocked when she finds out she went home with his twin!

#842 DEEP FOCUS
From Every Angle
by Erin McCarthy
Recently dumped and none-too-happy, Melanie Ambrose is stuck at a resort with Hunter Ryan, a bodyguard hired by her ex. Could a sexy fling with this virtual stranger cure her blues?

REQUEST YOUR FREE BOOKS!
2 FREE NOVELS PLUS 2 FREE GIFTS!

HARLEQUIN®
Blaze®
red-hot reads!

YES! Please send me 2 FREE Harlequin® Blaze™ novels and my 2 FREE gifts (gifts are worth about $10). After receiving them, if I don't wish to receive any more books, I can return the shipping statement marked "cancel." If I don't cancel, I will receive 4 brand-new novels every month and be billed just $4.74 per book in the U.S. or $4.96 per book in Canada. That's a savings of at least 14% off the cover price. It's quite a bargain. Shipping and handling is just 50¢ per book in the U.S. and 75¢ per book in Canada.* I understand that accepting the 2 free books and gifts places me under no obligation to buy anything. I can always return a shipment and cancel at any time. Even if I never buy another book, the two free books and gifts are mine to keep forever.

150/350 HDN F4WC

Name   (PLEASE PRINT)

Address   Apt. #

City   State/Prov.   Zip/Postal Code

Signature (if under 18, a parent or guardian must sign)

Mail to the **Harlequin® Reader Service:**
IN U.S.A.: P.O. Box 1867, Buffalo, NY 14240-1867
IN CANADA: P.O. Box 609, Fort Erie, Ontario L2A 5X3

Want to try two free books from another line?
Call 1-800-873-8635 or visit www.ReaderService.com.

* Terms and prices subject to change without notice. Prices do not include applicable taxes. Sales tax applicable in N.Y. Canadian residents will be charged applicable taxes. Offer not valid in Quebec. This offer is limited to one order per household. Not valid for current subscribers to Harlequin Blaze books. All orders subject to credit approval. Credit or debit balances in a customer's account(s) may be offset by any other outstanding balance owed by or to the customer. Please allow 4 to 6 weeks for delivery. Offer available while quantities last.

Your Privacy—The Harlequin® Reader Service is committed to protecting your privacy. Our Privacy Policy is available online at www.ReaderService.com or upon request from the Harlequin Reader Service.

We make a portion of our mailing list available to reputable third parties that offer products we believe may interest you. If you prefer that we not exchange your name with third parties, or if you wish to clarify or modify your communication preferences, please visit us at www.ReaderService.com/consumerschoice or write to us at Harlequin Reader Service Preference Service, P.O. Box 9062, Buffalo, NY 14269. Include your complete name and address.

HB13R2

SPECIAL EXCERPT FROM

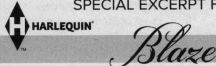

HARLEQUIN®

Blaze

Military veteran Mia Brandt agrees to a fake engagement to help sexy rescue swimmer Tag Johnson out of a jam. But could their fun, temporary liaison lead to something more?

Read on for a sneak preview at
WICKED SECRETS by **Anne Marsh**,
part of our UNIFORMLY HOT! miniseries.

Sailor boy didn't look up. Not because he didn't notice the other woman's departure—something about the way he held himself warned her he was aware of everyone and everything around him—but because polite clearly wasn't part of his daily repertoire.

Fine. She wasn't all that civilized herself.

The blonde made a face, her ponytail bobbing as she started hoofing it along the beach. "Good luck with that one," she muttered as she passed Mia.

Oookay. Maybe this *was* mission impossible. Still, she'd never failed when she'd been out in the field, and all her gals wanted was intel. She padded into the water, grateful for the cool soaking into her burning soles. The little things mattered so much more now.

"I'm not interested." Sailor boy didn't look up from the motor when she approached, a look of fierce concentration creasing his forehead. Having worked on more than one Apache helicopter during her two tours of duty, she knew the repair work wasn't rocket science.

She also knew the mechanic and…holy hotness.

Mentally, she ran through every curse word she'd learned. Tag Johnson hadn't changed much in five years. He'd acquired a few more fine lines around the corners of his eyes, possibly from laughing. Or from squinting into the sun since rescue swimmers spent plenty of time out at sea. The white scar on his forearm was as new as the lines, but otherwise he was just as gorgeous and every bit as annoying as he'd been the night she'd picked him up at the Star Bar in San Diego. He was also still out of her league, a military bad boy who was strong, silent, deadly…and always headed out the door.

For a brief second, she considered retreating. Unfortunately, the bridal party was watching her intently, clearly hoping she was about to score on their behalf. Disappointing them would be a shame.

"Funny," she drawled. "You could have fooled me."

Tag's head turned slowly toward her. Mia had hoped for drama. Possibly even his butt planting in the ocean from the surprise of her reappearance. No such luck.

"Sergeant Dominatrix," he drawled back.

Don't miss
WICKED SECRETS
by New York Times *bestselling author Anne Marsh,*
available April 2015 wherever
Harlequin® Blaze® books and ebooks are sold.

www.Harlequin.com

Love the Harlequin book you just read?

Your opinion matters.

Review this book on your favorite
book site, review site, blog or your own
social media properties and share
your opinion with other readers!

JUST CAN'T GET ENOUGH?

Join our social communities
and talk to us online.

You will have access to the latest
news on upcoming titles and special
promotions, but most importantly,
you can talk to other fans about your
favorite Harlequin reads.

Harlequin.com/Community

Facebook.com/HarlequinBooks

Twitter.com/HarlequinBooks

Pinterest.com/HarlequinBooks

HARLEQUIN®

A *Romance* FOR EVERY MOOD™

Stay up-to-date on all your
romance-reading news with the
Harlequin Shopping Guide,
featuring bestselling authors, exciting new
miniseries, books to watch and more!

The newest issue will be delivered right to you
with our compliments! There are 4 each year.

Signing up is easy.

EMAIL

ShoppingGuide@Harlequin.ca

WRITE TO US

HARLEQUIN BOOKS
Attention: Customer Service Department
P.O. Box 9057, Buffalo, NY 14269-9057

OR PHONE

1-800-873-8635 in the United States
1-888-343-9777 in Canada

Please allow 4-6 weeks for delivery of the first issue by mail.